AEP Urban Fiction
and
Hood Salidafied Publications
Presents

Brooklyn Sexy
2
A New Beginning

Myles Ramzee and Niko

MYLES RAMZEE

Brooklyn Sexy
All Right Reserved.
Copyright © 2015 Myles Ramzee and Niko
Cover Design by Angela Stevenson-Ringo

Angel Eyes Publications
P.O. Box 22031 Beachwood, Ohio 44122
angeleyespublications@yahoo.com

ISBN-13: 978-0692314739
ISBN-10: 0692314733
LCCN: 2014919891

AEP Urban Fiction is a Division of Angel Eyes Publications

MYLES RAMZEE

Chapter 1

Liz

Six months later

"I don't care what anybody says that boy Ne-Yo is gay."

"Hater....! He already proved he wasn't." The Ne-Yo basher's comment was met with words of anger, frustration and opinions of other customers inside the salon.

"You see that's the problem with black people. Every time one of us makes it people always wanna slander. They did it to Whitney, P-Diddy and what's that green eyed rappers name from back in the day?" Deidre commented with a question.

"Erick Sermon," Liz answered.

"Yeah him. Now they are doing it to Ne-Yo." As they spoke Ne-Yo's voice filled the salon from the flat screen T.V. tuned into B.E.T.

"Remember they said that about Eddie Murphy?" a guy getting his hair cut asked. Grunts and looks of skepticism filled the room and after a brief pause someone blurted, "The jury still out on that one. That transvestite thing is a little suspect." There was chuckles and laughter in the salon.

The conversation in the salon changed from various topics. Some of the topics became heated and intense topics ranging from the war in Iraq, to who was responsible for 9-11, and some people saying George Bush while others blamed Bin Laden and even Jewish people. "They said a bunch of Jews ain't show up for work that day. That's fishy."

"I bet you a lot of lazy ass black folk ain't show up for work that day either does that mean some black man was behind it?" someone blurted. When the discussion came up on Hurricane Katrina there was no argument or debate everyone agreed when someone commented. "Kanye West was right, the way they responded to that was a disgrace. George Bush doesn't care about black people."

"You know they're saying Kanye is gay too." That caused laughter to erupt from everyone. Liz sat in a barber chair facing the door when surprisingly Web walked in the shop. His large diamond pinky ring and earring sparkled as the light in the salon reflected off the diamonds creating a rainbow effect off the body. The shop became silent except for the T. V. now blasting 50 cents amusement park video. When Deidre saw him, also sitting in an empty chair, this was one time she was glad Diondre was not there. Web walked to a chair situated closed to the back of the store where a dark skinned male barber stood behind his chair.

"Web what's good my dude?" the barber greeted.

"Okay playboy I see cutting hair in Sing Sing landed you a job in the free world," Web said removing his red and white Phillies baseball cap taking a seat.

"No doubt." The barber said placing the barbershop apron over Web. Web removed his .45 from his waistband while the apron covered him. Then he mumbled to the barber.

"Don't turn me away from the door. Keep me facing it." The barber did as he was told.

Web smiled at Deidre "Wassup Deidre. Yeah this joint is popping," Web said then he smiled at Liz. Just as he was going to say something to Liz, in walks Jabbar. Liz jumped out of the chair to greet Jabbar with a kiss. Web stared at her butt in the tight Seven jeans.

"Hey Liz where your girl Debby at I ain't seen her in a while and why she ducking me?" Web asked grinning.

"How you doing Web I haven't heard from Debby in a minute," Liz greeted, and then answered Web while holding Jabbar's hand.

"Oh I'm chilling. Just tryna dodge the rumors floating around and stay out of trouble,"Web said with a hint of sarcasm in his tone.

"That's good, but nah I haven't heard from Debby," Liz repeated facing Jabbar. "So how you been baby. Where you coming from?" Liz faced Jabbar standing on her tiptoes to hug him around the neck. Web kept his eyes on Liz backside.

He started imagining his long manhood penetrating Liz's pretty haired pussy. He pictured his cream squirting on her cream-colored skin. He felt the weight of his gun against his developing erection.

"Damn, Liz you really doing a thing to them

Seven jeans. Homeboy must be tapping that good. Not like this thing I'm packing would." Web said looking at Liz as if he wanted to jump her bones right there on the spot.

Liz face became red with anger. She couldn't believe Web would disrespect her like that in front of Jabbar or in front of anyone period.

"Web don't do that, we better than that. I never disrespected you and we always been aiight." Liz grumbled.

"No disrespect ma. I'm just saying my man rock from Linden Projects showed me some nice flicks of you when I was up north and I just want to let you know that your body is all that.

And I would love to show it my gratitude," Web said with a mischievous grin.

"Check this homey. You're not gonna sit here and disrespect my fiancee in front of me. I suggest you show her and these people respect," Jabbar snorted while Liz held his arm.

"Baby its cool. It ain't worth it," Liz mumbled to Jabbar. Liz's heart began to pound when she saw the expression on Web's face turn to ice.

"I don't think you know who you talking to Duke and I'm not your homey. So sit yo pretty ass down before I help you do it," Web snarled putting his finger on the trigger of his gun unbeknown to everyone in the store. Still Liz didn't want Jabbar getting into a confrontation with Web. Web was a guy Liz knew that if you had a beef with, you would have to kill him or he'd kill you, and she didn't see Jabbar as a killer nor did she want him to be one though. She was turned on by him stepping up to her defense. A courageous man turns a woman on. Liz walked Jabbar out of the salon. "Betta tell that nigga something Liz before I violate my parole on his ass." Web threatened.

Deidre walked up close to Web's chair with an angry expression. "Web you were out of line. Liz has always been a friend to you, so why would you front on her like that?"

"Cmon Dee you know just as well as I know the bitch putting shit up in Debby head running her mouth like all these other gossiping people in these projects. Mufucka got something to say about Web say it to Web. Don't sit in a barbershop and have barbershop gossip about Web feel me!" Web barked eyeing other people in the shop.

Deidre sucked her teeth replying, "Web FYI you're not that important for us to be sitting here talking about you. So wherever you got that bright idea from take it back because that check bounced." Web laughed then mimicked Deidre "F.Y.I - F.Y.I. You done got real upper class whitey on me huh? You move out the projects with your Theo Huxtable boyfriend and now you telling me I'm not important. Nah Dee I am important. Ya'll just forgot, well I'm here to remind ya'll."

His hair was finished being cut just as he spoke his last words. Deidre stood there feeling as if she were slapped. She was at a loss for words. She didn't know how to view Web's sudden animosity towards Liz and herself. She thought better than to respond. A response could pro-long the argument and there is no telling what would come out of Web's mouth.

If Diondre walked in things would probably get ugly. Deidre didn't want that and she definitely didn't want Diondre possibly finding out that she once messed with a guy like Web.

She watched Web pay the barber then give the barber a handshake. "Don't let these gossiping mufuckas drag you in their bullshit. I'll holla."

Later that night Liz sat in her apartment still infuriated by Web's insults and disrespect.

Ever since she knew Web, they had always been on good terms with each other. When Web and Debby use to have fights before Web went to prison, Web would always consult Liz for Liz to mediate a make-up between him and Debby. Liz would talk to Debby for him telling Debby that Web was sorry and he wanted to make up. Debby would listen and her and Web would make up.

Web was always grateful to Liz for her help. He showed his gratitude a lot of times Web would give Liz a gift. Usually a piece of jewelry he caught from a victim of one of his robberies. Between Debby and Liz they had enough jewelry to open up their own jewelry shop.

Sometimes as a show of gratitude for the Jewelry, Liz would give Web clothes that she boosted without charge. Web had clothes for days due to Liz's and Debby's sticky fingers.

"You letting him win by dwelling on that non-sense baby," Jabbar said while he had Liz between his legs laying her on his chest massaging her shoulders as they sat on the couch.

"I just don't like anyone coming at me like I did something to them when all I ever did was be a friend. I never ever disrespect Web. And he gonna to talk to..." Liz sighed and sucked her teeth not finishing her sentence. Jabbar massage started to ease the tension and he hit a spot that let a soft moan escape from her breath.

"You know what will make me forget about earlier?" Liz asked Jabbar leaning her head back looking up at him a sexy, seductive voice.

"What's that?" he asked returning a seductive tone.

"I need you to take my clothes off and fuck me like it's our last fuck," Liz said aggressively.

Jabbar happily obliged Liz's request. In return, Liz turned up her freak game. She allowed Jabbar to give her some hard anal work and a golden shower. Turned on by her freakiness Jabbar got freaky and let Liz orally please his brown hole.

When Jabbar was on the verge of releasing his juices, Liz groaned, "Cum on my face!"

Jabbar ejaculated a heavy load on her face.

"AAAH Yeah!" Liz smeared the liquid on her face while licking the rest off her fingers. They continued this sexcapade in the showers, the kitchen floor the living room and every other part of the apartment until the wee hours of the night. When they finally came up for air, winded and exhausted all they both could utter was "Wow!"

Deidre lay in bed while Diondre was at his computer reviewing the stock market on the internet, not as infuriated as Liz was, but wondering if she had changed to the point that she's acting snobbish. Webs comment that she sounded uppity bothered her. She didn't want to appear as the type of person who made it out of the ghetto and looked down on those who haven't had the opportunity to escape. Deidre always knew how to speak correct English in a proper manner so she ignored the comments a lot of black people, who couldn't hold a conversation that could save their lives, made when you spoke correctly that you were speaking white. People didn't realize that by making that statement what they're actually saying is that black people talk as if their dumb, justifying the ridiculous, absurd white supremacist notion that black people are intellectually inferior to whites.

It's another thing to act as if you're superior to your own people because of your economic status. That is something that looked upon with distaste. So Web's insult struck a nerve. To get her mind off Web's antics she interrupted Diondre's on-line activity. "You going be on that computer all night or are you gonna come over here and get some of this good shit," she said in her most ghettofied voice pulling up her negligee spreading her legs rubbing her shaved an exposed middle.

Diondre stared at the computer. "The Dow, the Nasdaq and the S and P are all up..." He turned his head while talking and paused when he saw Deidre playing with herself, biting her lip and giving him the come fuck me look. He quickly removed his cotton Polo pajamas and skipped over to the bed.

"Girl you ain't saying nothing but a thing."

***

The driver of the Dodge magnum stopped at a gas station on Bedford and Atlantic Avenue. Before he got out to pay twenty dollars to the clerk for gas he answered his cell phone.

"Speak," he mumbled.

"It's me yo," the voice of Web said into his ears.

"So what's the verdict on that thing you were telling me about. Is it on or what?"

"Yeah that's going down. It's moving a little slow cause the target ain't been reached yet.

But don't sweat it though son. The right moves is being made feel me," Web replied.

"Yo son that thing in the Bronx got messy I meant to tell you about that a while back. Big nigga tried..."

"No need to dwell that's the pass. Plus son told me the whole Shabang. Shit happens though. Listen I'm not gonna talk long. As soon as my people is in we in. One."

The guy with the Dodge magnum walked to the clerk's booth and slid a twenty dollar bill through a slot. Twenty on three!" the guy yelled. When he turned to walk back to his car he was met by the sound of the two white men, one in an outdoor flannel shirt and the other with a USC sweatshirt pointing guns at him. "Don't move or I blow your head off. Put your hands on your head!" the guy looked in shock as cars with lights flashing on dashboards came to halts with swarms of detectives jumping out. As he was being cuffed, a cop yelled to another cop.

"Yeah this is him, can't stop doing burglaries homey. Just invite yourself to peoples stuff?" the cop asked sarcastically mocking the words of street thugs.

Dodge Magnum shook his head looking down at the ground. "I got nothing to say. Get me a lawyer."

When Dodge Magnum was brought to the precinct, he was escorted into a tiny cell. The walls were littered with writing that were a testament of the many people that were caged there one time or another. The smell of old urine and funk also seconded that notion. There was a large sign on the door printed in military style print that read, "If you help the inspectors, they will help you." Five minutes after being placed in the cell Dodge Magnum, handcuffed to a pole sitting on a bench, watched as two plain clothes cop walked in the cell. One cop looked to be Hispanic, his dark hair and swarthy skin gave Dodge Magnum that impression to him the cop looked like an eighties version of the Spanish cop off the TV show Chips. The other cop was a young Johnny Depp wannabe with clothes that fit him to tight.

The Spanish cop held out a pack of Newport's to Dodge Magnum, which he immediately grabbed. The Johnny Depp look-a-like lit the cigarette for him. Dodge Magnum held in his laugh. He knew the routine with cops and their interrogation tactics. He knew they were trying to make him feel comfortable for when they start requesting information. The prisoner would spill his guts. This was something he been through plenty of times. He wasn't going to turn down a smoke though.

"So Mister Gaston you're a pretty famous man around these parts." The fake Johnny Depp said.

"You got a lot of people that want to interview you." He continued.

"The FBI, cops out of the Bronx, what you been up to?" the Spanish cop cut in.

Mister Gaston thought to himself; *wish they would cut the bullshit and get to the point. Hold up FBI and cops from the Bronx? Ah man here come the bullshit.*

"All we wanna know is about the burglaries in Brooklyn and who's your partner or partners." The Spanish cop asked.

The expression on Gaston's face made his dark skinned forehead wrinkle.

"I thought once I request a lawyer the sixth amendment is an affect. So why are ya'll here?"

Gaston's question made the expression on the detectives face appears as if someone smacked them silly. As they begin to walk out of the cell Gaston added insult to injury by sarcastically blurting.

"Oh and thanks for the smokes Johnny Depp and Poncharell."

Gaston sighed when three other dicks walked in. Two wore clean suits that looked a little to pressed and tailored. The other cop looked like the old Colombo type. Gaston knew it was the cop from the Bronx. Most likely homicide and the suits were definitely the feds. Gaston's suspicions were confirmed when the suits, both white men that looked to be in their early forties, flashed their gold badges with the FBI insignia.

"Mister Gaston, we're federal agents and this is a homicide detective out of the Bronx.

We know you lawyer up so we won't ask any questions..." one of the suits said reaching in a manila envelope dropping what look like surveillance photos.

"What we will do is show you some things and if you want to explain feel free. The detective from the Bronx is here about this." A surveillance photo showing Gaston entering Cornbread's Co-op city apartment building was displayed in the agent's hand.

The Bronx cop cut in. "Through a long process of elimination you're the only person that entered the building that day none of the tenants know." The Bronx cop showed Gaston a picture of Cornbread's body lying in a pool of blood then continued.

"This happened around the time you were seen leaving the building." Gaston knew it was all circumstantial so he said nothing and then the feds dropped a bomb.

"See Mister Gaston we're in the know. We know that you went into this apartment to burglarize it. That's what you do. Your fingerprints match ones found at burglaries in Connecticut and New Jersey.

We've been looking for you. You weren't alone though. Someone else entered that apartment before you, possibly through the outside. They entered through the terrace. The apartment is a second floor apartment so that was easy. We could have been had you but we put a tail on you and you were seen here."

The agent showed Gaston a picture of him picking up a package under the elevated L train on Livonia Avenue. Gaston swallowed.

"A confidential informant told us that that was the drop for the kidnap for ransom of Ty-Ran Clarkson. A ten year old and the son of this man..." the agent showed a mug-shot of Ty-Ran.

"We don't know who was behind the plot or who the kidnappers were but we got you picking up the money and the person that put the money there has confirmed that she put it there. So you are the only person that's gonna be held accountable for the kidnapping."

"Buddy you looking at twenty years minimum with us and possibly life in the state. You can help yourself out of this. You gotta play ball man," the agent said to a now sweating Gaston.

The agents knew they were making a break through when a tear rolled down Gaston's cheek.

With a trembling lip Gaston spoke. "Listen I'm a homosexual and 1 was led into this by my lover. His nickname, I don't know his real one is...

Chapter 2

Deidre

Richmond, Virginia

"This is Richmond's number one station for Hip Hop and R&B. Don't forget tonight at the Satellite their hosting a hair show. Ladies you don't wanna miss it...."

Deidre and Liz listened to the radio as they unpacked their luggage inside the double bedded room at a Best Western Hotel in Richmond Virginia.

"These country chicks ain't got anything on us Dee. I'm telling you those bama ass hairdo's are not cute," Liz remarked.

Deidre smiled at Liz as she removed a pair of jeans out of her suitcase.

"I wouldn't be so quick to judge. There are people here from all over. D.C, Philly, Jersey and those are places where they specialize in hair," Deidre said matter of factly.

"I don't care about those places, I'm from Brooklyn and we're the best."

Deidre didn't want to shatter Liz's confidence or hers either, so she gave a boost in spirit.

"You damn right we are. Let's show them how to do this BK style girl."

Before Liz and Deidre left the hotel, they stopped by the rooms of girls that would model the hairstyles that Deidre, Liz and other girls in the salon did. The models were also from Brooklyn and were customers of D and D's salon and cuts. Deidre and Liz prep talk the girls for the show, and like a team in the huddle Deidre excitedly cheered.

"Ladies lets show these bitches how it's really done!"

"Aiight I hear that."

The women toured Richmond for a while before the hair show. The models went shopping in downtown Richmond for outfits to wear as they modeled their hairdos. While at the restaurant, Liz had a thought. She didn't express it to Deidre because she knew Deidre's jolly mood would turn sour. Liz excused herself from the table to step outside and dial a number on her cell phone. When Liz heard a female voice that had a heavy country accent she asked, "Hello is Debby there?"

"No baby may I ask whose speaking?" the woman asked kindly. In the background, Liz could hear a baby crying and the sound of screaming kids.

"Boy sit yo ass down!" The woman on the phone yelled.

"I'm a friend of Debby's from New York. I wanted to let her know I was in town," Liz said.

The voiced that yelled at the child switch back to the cordial voice that answered the phone. "Baby she went with her New York boyfriend to get some clothes. She gonna be at the hair show down at Satellite. You probably in town for that huh?"

Boyfriend from New York? Who the hell Debby got down here from New York that's her boyfriend! Probably some nigga from New York that came down here to hustle. Debby don't waste any time, Liz thought to herself.

"Yes ma'am that's what I'm here for," Liz answered.

"You'll see Debby there tonight now."

"Okay thank you." Liz ended the call. Just as she was about to go back in the restaurant she remembered to make one more call. After dialing the number and upon hearing Jabbar's sexy voice Liz smiled. A smile that could be seen from a block away.

"Hey lover boy," Liz said in a sexy tone.

"What's up baby girl? I was just about to call you and let you know I'm leaving tonight. I might not catch the show but I'll be there to be with you. I'ma try to be there for the show but I gotta make a run. Take pictures just in case." Jabbar said.

Liz put on a sad face. "Aw baby I wanted you to see the show," she said in a baby voice.

"I know baby something came up with a client. I'm sorry but I'm going to try and make it to the show,"

"Well alright. I'll see you when you get here. Love you," Liz grumbled in a surrendering voice.

"Love you Liz."

"Love you too."

Back at the table Deidre was smiling at Liz as she took a seat.

"Girl you are sprung," Deidre joked.

Liz made a face as if she were confused about what Deidre was saying. "What are you talking bout?"

Deidre frowned. "Heeere you go frontin. I know you called Jabbar. You just got off the phone with him in the hotel." Deidre shook her head smiling.

"So..." Liz sucked her teeth. "You were like that when you first got with Diondre. Especially after ya'll first did the nasty. You came to school cheesing telling me that he made you cum like eight times before he bust his first one. You was open."

Deidre looked embarrassed. "Girl shut yo mouth, you talking all loud," Deidre looked around to see if any of the diners were looking at them.

Liz leaned in closer. "Bitch please ain't any of these country people thinking about our up north asses. Don't be calling me sprung," Liz said with a smile before continuing. "Plus I came like ten times before Jabbar got his first one off."

"Daaaamn!" Deidre growled. She covered her mouth embarrassed that she drew attention with her outburst. Some of the people looked, then seeing there was no emergency return their attention back to their own tables.

"Ten times? Girl you done hit pay dirt. I haven't had that happen since high school," Deidre said. "Matter fact I don't think I ever came that much."

"Girl I'm talking that many times from the dick. With his mouth I damn near jumped out the window. I must have come almost fifteen times, back to back one after the other." Liz boasted.

"You're lying? Girl I can't even do that with my friend with batteries," Deidre said referring to her vibrator.

"Shit girl when Jabbar practically moved in my apartment. I gave my friend with batteries an eviction notice," Liz joked. She and Deidre howled in laughter.

In a make shift dressing room which was really in the back of the club. Liz and Deidre ran from model to model in a nervous attempt to make sure the hairdos were tight and nothing was out of place. They sprayed, curled even clipped hair that was already done before the show started.

Once the show started, Deidre and Liz took seats in front of the make shift stage next to other competitors from around the country. Liz and Deidre watched nervously as girls from other shops around the country walked on stage showing off their hairstyles. Liz laughed at some of the hairdo's she saw, at the same time she had to admit to herself a lot of the sisters that walked out had hairdo's that were amazing and it made her and Deidre more nervous. When Deidre was in college, she attended hair shows as part of her course in Cosmetology. Deidre already knew that the competition would be fierce. This was all new to Liz.

The girls from D and D's were finally announced. "Ladies and Gentlemen, from Brooklyn New York, welcome the ladies of D and D hair salon and cuts!" Liz and Deidre held on to each other smiling and nervous.

The girls looked good and they put on a good

show. Liz exhaled after it seem like she held her breath through D and D's whole time on stage.

"Dee I got to pee. My nerves are ready to explode. I'll be back," Liz said walking off. As Liz walked to the bathroom, she spotted Debby coming out of the bathroom holding a drink in her hand.

"Debby wassup girl!" Liz yelled excitedly holding her arms open inviting Debby to a hug.

"Hey Liz wassup baby! I was wondering where you were. I saw your girls they looked real good. I'm proud of you," Debby said after hugging Liz. The girls gave each other the look over. Liz noticed that Debby looked a little thinner in the face but she still had the big caboose in her tight jeans. Debby had her hair in tight micro braids. Liz could tell Debby was a little tipsy.

"What you been up to Deb. Where's your son?" Liz enquired. After sipping from her straw, Debby slurred. "My friend is babysitting him for me. I got my own crib now. Oh and I got a job working at a restaurant downtown. I make eight dollars an hour plus tips."

"That's what's up I'm happy for you," Liz said. To Liz's dismay as her and Debby talked Liz couldn't believe who she saw walking in her direction. The sight of this person made Liz's stomach turn. What is he doing here? She then remembered the phone call she made earlier when she was looking for Debby.

"She's with her boyfriend from New York," Liz remembered Debby's friend saying. *I know dam well she wasn't talking about this bastard.*

"Oh shit Liz what up ma?" Web said as he walked up hugging Debby from behind.

Liz looked at Debby with a look of disbelief and disgust. Liz was definitely confused.

Debby read Liz look and looked down at her feet embarrassed.

"Ain't no wassup. Debby what is you doing with this nigga?" Liz growled at Debby.

The grin on Web's face disappeared. "Deb ain't got to explain nothing to you. Who is you her psychiatrist or something?"

"Chill Web..." Debby said facing Web. "Liz let me holla at you," Debby grabbed Liz hand and pulled her towards the ladies bathroom.

"Uh uh Debby I know damn well you ain't fucking with this clown after all you been through. I thought you left New York to get away from him and start over." Liz barked.

"I did but I found out he had nothing to do with my son's kidnapping. I found out a lot of shit Liz." Debby said.

"Like what and from who?" Liz asked in a tone that sounded as if she really needed some hard evidence to prove that Web wasn't somehow involved. Debby explained that the FBI showed her a picture of the guy who picked the money up from the Livonia station that she dropped off. They told her that a confidential informant out of Red Hook projects told them about the kidnapping. They asked Debby did she know the guy which Debby said she didn't.

They explained he was a Bronx man convicted of burglaries in the past. His prison record said that he was a known homosexual and he is H.I.V infected. Debby didn't show the agents how she was feeling with that news. Hearing that Web was an alleged homo made her think he might have H.I.V and possibly gave it to her. Debby went and got tested and the test was negative. That made her doubt the validity of Web being a homosexual. The guy in the picture couldn't have been Web's lover or Web would have the disease was Debby's rationale.

They also informed her that he was the man responsible for the murder of her friend Cornbread. The guy was an associate of Cornbread in a burglary ring. Cornbread, they think, owed the guy some money and refused to pay. That was speculation on their part. To Debby though, that meant that Web wasn't involved.

Her feeling guilty of accusing him made her call him and apologize. The N.Y.P.D offered to pay for her protection because the guy was on the loose and maybe would be after Debby and her son. They gave Debby money to purchase a house in Virginia.

Debby accepted. Debby also asked Web to take a H.I.V test, which he complied to and was found to be negative.

Liz listened to Debby story still not convinced that Web was totally innocent in his involvement. Her anger came from more of the fact that Web disrespected her in the salon. When Liz told Debby about the incident all Debby said was, "He was just angry. He heard rumors and you know how ya'll talk in the shop."

Liz face got red and her blood boiled and without thinking. Slap! Debby held her face in disbelief and shock Liz would dare to put her hands on her. Liz walked away fuming. She was so angry that she forgot what type of girl Debby was. Debby wasn't the type of girl you hit and walked away from. No, Debby is still a Brooklyn girl to the heart. Liz didn't see it coming.

She just felt her hair get pulled making her fall backwards looking up at Debby's fist coming towards her face.

"Fight!" someone yelled turning everyone attention towards Debby and Liz.

"That's right baby, fuck that bitch up," Web cheered Debby on.

Debby was too strong for Liz. Liz could not get up. She scratched and clawed at Debby's hand but Debby wouldn't let go of her hair. Debby sat on top of Liz and punched Liz repeatedly on the face and neck.

"Bitch...Don't-you-ever-put-yo-hands-on me," Debby mumbled between punches. Blood leaked from Liz nose and lip.

Deidre remembering that Liz went to the bathroom ran over making her way through the crowd. When she saw Debby and Liz fighting and Web standing there, Deidre became confused.

In a quick move, she grabbed her cell phone and smashed it against Debby's ear, causing Debby to grab her ear in pain.

"Ahh!" Debby yelled falling to the floor dizzy. Web grabbed Deidre from behind and threw her to the ground. When he turned back around to see if Debby was fine, Liz was on top of Debby wailing away. Liz was punching and kicking Debby hard on her face with the high heel shoe she wore. Debby's ear and lips were bleeding heavily. A gash appeared on her cheek bone as the heel of Liz shoe grazed her face.

"Web get her off me!" Debby pleaded.

Bouncers outside the club ran in and held Web, Liz and Deidre while another helped Debby off the floor. Web tried to break loose but the bouncer was huge and too strong. The club owner didn't want to draw negative attention to the events so he had his bouncers escort Liz and Deidre to their car while the other security personnel did the same for Web and Debby.

Back at the hotel Liz packed her bags while Deidre sat on the bed staring at Liz.

"Liz just wait until tomorrow. They're gonna announce the winners. We got to be there," Deidre said.

"Look at my face Dee. Do you think I'm showing up looking like this huh? Hell no I ain't. You stay I'm outta here." Liz said through swollen lips, steaming mad.

Deidre shook her head. She would have done the same thing if she were Liz. Deidre didn't want to be there by herself when they announced the winner of the hair show. Yeah she had the girls who modeled but Deidre wanted to celebrate with her best friend.

"Dee if I stay I'm going fuck around and catch

a case on Debby's ass. I swear if I ever see her in New York I'm a cut the shit out of her face!" Liz left Virginia that night forgetting that Jabbar was on his way there.

***

After receiving four stitches on her face and two on her ear; Debby with Web by her side; left a Richmond emergency room.

"Yo these bitches are out of their rabbit ass minds thinking they goin come at me like I'm some soft ass bitch. They lucky I couldn't get in that joint with my razor or I would have tore they asses up." Debby snorted as Web drove off in his jeep.

"Don't sweat that ma. That bitch Liz gonna remember that ass whoopin you put on her." Web said trying to put Debby at ease.

"Oooh and this bitch Deidre she goin hit me with a phone. Yo that bitch I swear on my son I'm a get her." Debby felt the bandage in her ear and face and grew angrier. She knew that it made Deidre feel good. Deidre always wanted revenge for the beating she received at the hands of Debby in high school. Deidre did get a euphoric feeling when she sent Debby wincing in pain from her blow. What Debby didn't know was that before Deidre swung the phone, the day Debby beat Deidre up flashed in Deidre's mind and that motivated Deidre into swinging that phone with all the strength she had.

"Don't sweat her ma. I got something in store for her and that Theo Huxtable nigga," Web said with a sinister grin.

Debby looked over at Web skeptically. The look on his face said that he was up to something devious and Debby knew who he was referring to when he said Theo Huxtable. He called Diondre that, comparing him to the character on the Cosby show; clean pretty boy who lived in the upper class life in Brooklyn.

Diondre had nothing to do with what happened at the show. Debby didn't want to start having suspicious thoughts about Web again but the look on his face made her unsure of his innocence involving matters of the past. Debby decided to let it go for now.

Chapter 3

Deidre

Her entire life flashed in her mind as she laid on her stomach with a pillow positioned under it feeling her insides being filled making her body feel pleased beyond her wildest dream.

"Yes this feels so right oh god this is so wrong. Please don't stop!' she moaned as his hardness touched the very essence of her being. She felt her vaginal walls soaked with her own juices as she contracted her muscles to grip his love organ.

What flashed in her mind was a collage of past and present events in her now even more complicated life. Her childhood, running around her project apartment in a walker being lifted by her handsome father, to her first kiss in the playground as she climbed the top of the monkey bars in a game of run, catch and kiss. Then her mind replayed her lying on her back in the bed of her first lover. She remembered the pain of the experience, which eventually turned into pleasure. "Oh yes baby fuck me. Fuck me so good!"

Switching positions looking at him from the missionary position her mind was still flashed to her high school days walking happily through the halls with her sweetheart. His face was so handsome she remembered. His lovemaking came to her vision along with the proposal.

"This pussy is yours oh yes this is yours uhhh!"

Her mind filled with guilt that her body betrayed. Her mind was thinking *what am I doing? Why am I here letting someone else's man make love to me? My best friend's man! Oh God but it feels so good.* She grabbed his back then scratched it as she felt the ninth orgasm coming from the core of her inner being.

"I'm cumin oh god I'm cumin!" she blurted. His rhythm switched and she knew he was on the verge of releasing his body fluid. "Aah shit!" he grunted as his liquid entered her insides. Both of them laid on their backs soaked in sweat. She couldn't believe what just happened.

What type of friend am I that I would do something like this? Deidre's mind did a rewind of the past couple of hours that led up to her laying in a Virginia hotel room having the most sweat-filled, ecstatic, no holds barred, freaky sex she had in a while with her best friend's fiancé. As she replayed it in her mind, she looked over at Jabbar with a forced smile.

***

Liz boarded a plane at the Richmond airport wearing 70's style shades, the shades that covered most of her face. She wore a blue bandanna over her hair and sat at a window seat. By the time the plane was in the air Liz realized that while she was headed to New York Jabbar was mostly headed to Virginia.

She cursed herself for being in such a rage that she would forget that important fact. She couldn't contact him by phone because her minutes ran out.

"Oh god he is going to be pissed," she mumbled to herself.

Earlier that evening

Meanwhile Jabbar was on the arrivals deck of the airport waiting for the baggage handler to help bring his suitcase to the Hertz rental car he had. After tipping the skycap, Jabbar drove to the Best Western. He tried dialing Liz's phone but couldn't get through. He dialed the room but didn't get an answer. He was sure he missed the show but he decided to drive over to the place just in case.

As he drove by the Best Western he saw Deidre about to jump into a taxi. He rolled down his window and yelled out to her. Deidre told the taxi that she didn't need him and tipped him for his trouble. She ran over to the car with frustrated look on her face.

"Deidre wassup where you headed? Where's Liz?" Jabbar asked.

Deidre got in the car and sighed. "Jabbar it's a long story. I'm headed to the restaurant to get something to eat. C'mon I'll tell you the whole thing there." At the restaurant Deidre relayed the whole story to a stunned Jabbar.

"Wow. That is some crazy stuff. I know the

people at the show were like 'them crazy New Yorkers'," Jabbar said leaning back in the chair.

Deidre shook her head in disbelief. "Yeah I bet you their doing some New York bashing as we speak."

"Can you blame them? You know how ghetto Liz can get and that girl Debby..." Jabbar sighed before continuing. "Her picture is next to ghetto in the dictionary."

Deidre laughed. Deidre spent the rest of the dinner laughing and enjoying Jabbar's company. They talked about everything from the investment Diondre made, marriage, relationships, politics and even sex. When the conversation got to sex, Deidre was surprised of how open Jabbar was about the topic.

"A man should make sure a woman gets her thing off first cause a man's orgasm is automatic a woman's has to be in it mentally as well as physical in order to get good results.

It's all physical with guys. That's why I love foreplay, especially oral."

For some reason, Deidre felt comfortable talking to him about sex. He made her feel comfortable. After dinner, they walked around as the streets of Richmond became empty at night.

"If this was New York it still would have been noisy and jumping," Jabbar commented.

Deidre looked at her watch and saw that it was two in the morning.

"People just getting started in the city. Crazy place ain't it?" she said in a statement more than a question.

When the temperature got a little chilly, Jabbar noticed that Deidre had a thin blouse on and she looked cold. He offered his tan cotton Sean John blazer for her to wear. Deidre found the gesture to be sweet. She smiled at Jabbar as they walked. He smiled back. They walked in silence for a few more blocks both in their own thoughts. Deidre thought to herself. *If I don't get away from this beautiful man my marriage will be in jeopardy and my friendship with Liz. He smelled so damn good and boy is he easy on the eyes.*

Jabbar imagined him naked with her feeling her soft bottom against his manhood as they spooned after a session of energy draining sex. Jabbar broke the silence with, "I got that Kat Williams stand up DVD, let's have a movie night cap." Deidre liked that idea.

Not even a half hour into the movie as they both ate some ice cream did Jabbar take the pint of Ben and Jerry's out of her hand and kiss her. Initially Deidre became scared. Her heart began to pound she was telling herself to pull away don't let him do it but her lips said come on.

Her lips won the battle because her tongue and lips met his and she could taste the chunky monkey ice cream on his tongue. His lips were as soft as she imagined and she moaned as his lips went to her neck.

He slowly removed her blouse and lace bra softly massaging her erect brown nipples.

Deidre inhaled and exhaled as his touch made

her skin goose bump. She helped him remove his clothing feeling the hardness of his muscular body that made her middle tingle with wetness.

They kissed passionately as they both got naked on the bed. Deidre rubbed his body from his chest, past his six-packed stomach to his throbbing hardness; with tenderness, she stroked him causing him to release a soft moan from his throat.

Deidre still stroking him begin to suck his nipple. She licked down to his belly button slow and graceful. Her teasing made Jabbar more turned on in anticipation of what was next.

With her tongue still cold from the ice cream, she took Jabbar in her mouth causing him to arch his back and moan. She massaged his balls while licking the top of his manhood wet from precum. She licks up and down his shaft slowly while moaning. She placed his balls in her mouth gently then moaned hard to create a vibration. Jabbar's toes almost broke from him curling them.

Jabbar didn't want to cum before he got to taste her and feel inside of her, so he took control.

He laid Deidre on her stomach and licked on her middle from behind. As he tickled her clit with his tongue Deidre buried her face in the pillow. Jabbar parted her soft golden plump cheeks and licked from her clit to her asshole. Deidre moaned into the pillow, which muffled the sound. Jabbar slapped her cheeks as he licked sending pleasurable sensations through Deidre's body. Each slap caused her to blurt out, "Oh yes Jabbar slap it hard. Harder!" Jabbar followed orders.

With her juices on his mouth and chin from her cummin at least ten times, Jabbar entered her in that position. Her nest gripped his rod pulling him in. Jabbar's eyes almost rolled up in his head when she did that. He had that done on plenty of occasions but Deidre had the strongest pull he had experienced. She almost sucked the life out of him with her pussy.

Jabbar pumped slow at first teasing Deidre as she gripped the sheets biting her bottom lip.

"Jabbar fuck me baby. Oh God I want you so bad. Fuck me Daddy!" Jabbar fastened his pace which made Deidre go wild in her moment of ecstasy.

"Yeah! Yeah! Yeah! Baby yeah! Faster! Faster! Oh yes!" she pants as he pumped faster and harder. Jabbar watched his manhood going in and out each time coming out wetter from her multiple orgasms.

They fucked in every position known to man.

Karma Sutra was now remixed with Jabbar and Deidre's rendezvous. They sometimes came together. She came on his pole, his face, while he came in her, on her ass cheeks, in her ass, as they engaged in anal something Deidre never did with Diondre. Something she knew she could get use to. She rubbed his cum on her breast while they took the sex into the shower. After it was all said and done, Deidre knew how it got to that point.

Deidre laid on the bed after thinking about what she did while Jabbar went into the hallway to get some ice. The guilt became more unbearable until a tear rolled down her face. She would have to talk to Jabbar. He had to know that she loved Diondre and she didn't want to ruin her friendship with Liz. They couldn't do this anymore. It was a one-time thing. It was a mistake.

A heavenly mistake she thought, but a mistake. There was a lot at stake and they'd have to put it behind them and never let it happen again. Deidre's mind flashed back to the few hours of some real good sex. The best she ever had and she couldn't believe that she was even contemplating trying to figure a way for them to do it again without getting caught. No! She told herself. This has to stop. She would tell Jabbar as soon as she came back.

She ran it through her mind what she would tell him. *Jabbar I think you the most beautiful man I ever laid eyes on and as much as I enjoyed what we just did, it can't happen again. It is wrong on both our parts and it will only hurt people we both love mutually. Liz is in love with you with all she has and I imagine you love her also. I've been in love with Diondre since high school and I love him just as much if not more today. So let's put this behind us and call it what it is sinful lust that got the best of us. It won't happen again.*

When Jabbar came back in the room Deidre smiled at him. He smiled back and they went at it for another two hours. After that session was done, Deidre took a shower alone while Jabbar watched the Kat Williams DVD.

When Deidre came out of the shower, she heard the sound of a woman moaning and screaming. "Yes, fuck me Jabbar!" it was coming from the TV the voice sounded awfully familiar to Deidre. When she looked at Jabbar he was watching the video with a sinister grin on his face. Deidre looked in utter dismay at her own image and acts staring at her from the TV.

"Jabbar what the fuck is that. How the ...?"

"Have a seat Deidre. We got a lot of talking to do..." Jabbar said tapping the bed gesturing for Deidre to sit down.

"You taped us. What is this about?" Deidre asked grabbing her robe all of a sudden feeling embarrassingly naked. Jabbar pointed to his carry-on bag that sat on a chair facing the bed. Deidre realized this is where he hid the camera.

"If you don't want this to get out this is what I need you to do."

Chapter 4

Diondre

When Liz got back to the city, she called Jabbar. He answered on the first ring.

"Wassup baby?" Jabbar said and to Liz's shock he didn't sound angry that she left Virginia before he got there. Liz knew that Deidre explained what happened and the understanding man he was he wouldn't be angry.

"Are you ok baby? Deidre told me everything," Jabbar consoled.

"Yeah I'm good. I'm even better now that you're not mad at me," Liz replied.

"I ain't gonna lie I was at first then I heard that mess and I would have did the same. Where you at?"

"I'm home. I just called Diondre and told him I have to take a week off, family business. I don't need him knowing what happened." Liz said.

"I feel you. Deidre was saying the same thing so we'll keep that on a hush. We're on our way home now. Oh I'm sorry baby but ya'll came in second. Next year ya'll get it though," Jabbar said in an attempt to liven up Liz's mood.

The hair show was the last thing on Liz's mind though. She still was appalled by Debby's actions. Liz couldn't understand how Debby could betray her like that. Liz was there for her through all the mess Debby was in, Liz still thinks because of Web but regardless of who was responsible for Debby's dilemma Liz was the one that reached out with a helping hand when no one else would and this is what she gets in return?

"Jabbar I need you here with me," Liz said.

"I'm on my way baby. I'll take care of you," Jabbar said in a sexy voice.

Though it hurt to smile Liz still did. "I know you will. Love you."

"Love you too," Liz ended the call.

Liz called out of work for a total of three weeks. In that time Deidre also took off from the shop. She complained of not feeling well. She woke up in the morning throwing up with a fever. She felt it was from the stress of her time in Virginia and the whole issue with Jabbar.

Diondre thought it was the flu. Deidre couldn't look Liz in the face and she didn't want to get intimate with Diondre cause she felt he might of sensed something. She heard men could tell if his woman had sex with another man because her vagina would feel different. Deidre didn't know how true that was but she wanted her stuff to tighten up before she let Diondre in again.

Then one night Diondre came in the house with a question that caught Deidre off balance.

"Why didn't you tell me that Liz had a fight at the hair show with that girl from the far side?"

Deidre laid in the bed drowsy from the Nyquil and Tylenols she took. "Liz didn't wanna talk about it. How did you find out?" Deidre said in a groggy voice.

"Did you forget ya'll bought girls down there with ya'll. Did you think loud mouth Layna was going keep it a secret when she came in the shop," Diondre snapped.

Deidre could have kicked herself. Why did she forget to tell the girls not to say anything?

How could she be so dumb? This Jabbar thang had gotten her off her square. She had to get it together.

"Liz didn't wanna talk about it, so why didn't you wanna talk about it with me?" Diondre inquired.

"Dre I didn't want you to make it seem bigger than what it was. They had an argument and it..."

Diondre cut her off. "Bigger than what it was. You had to bash her in the head with a cell phone, her boyfriend from the far side throws you on the floor, Liz face busted up and you gonna say bigger than what it was, Are you kidding me Deidre? This man put his hands on my fiance!"

"See Dre they over exaggerated. He held me, he didn't throw me," Deidre lied. The last thing she wanted was for Diondre to go looking for Web not realizing how much of a problem that would turn into. With Web, things could get way out of hand. She witness Web's brutality with her own eyes.

1994

"Beyond the walls of intelligence life is divine I think of crime when I'm in a New York state of mind." The voice of Nas roared from a radio where groups of teenagers sat on project benches. Deidre a nineteen year old at the time sat on the bench on the hot summer day with Liz and the other teens. Some bopped their head to Nas' description of the streets of the Big Apple while others laughed and talked.

"What made ya'll go to Jeff instead of Canarse High?" A girl with long braided extensions chewing gum, making smacking sounds with it as she talk, asked Liz and Deidre.

Deidre looked over at Liz and rolled her eyes. "Ask miss wanna fight everyone," Deidre said.

"Shut up Dee. I was beating that private house bitch up you ain't have to jump in," Liz shot back moving her head and neck as she spoke.

"It didn't look like you were winning that much to me.... Anyway," Deidre looked at the girl asking the question. "We got kicked out and sent to Jeff."

As they spoke suddenly, the sound of screeching tires could be heard followed by rapid gunfire. TAT! TAT! TAT! TAT! BRRRAT!

The teens on the bench all ducked, some crawled under benches or ran in buildings.

Deidre and Liz ducked under the bench. Deidre looked to see where the shots were coming from and she spotted a man in the passenger side of a dark colored car aiming a gun out the window firing at a person running at top speed. Deidre recognized the running man as Web. Deidre could feel her heart pounding in fear and even though Web broke her heart, for some reason she was praying that a bullet wouldn't strike him down.

Her prayers were answered. She saw Web hop over a fence and run towards Flatlands Avenue while the guy in the car kept driving down Glenwood road towards Pennsylvania Avenue. Then Deidre heard her mother's voice call out.

"Dee Dee gets up here now!"

Liz looked at Deidre as they crawled from under the bench and shrugged her shoulders.

"I'll see you later Liz," Deidre walked in the direction of the building. As she walked she looked up at a third floor window and seen Miss Evelyn, an old lady who lived in the projects since they were built in the 30's. She was one of the first black tenants. She moved from the south. Deidre read the expression on the old woman's face. To Deidre it was as if the old woman had the sounds of an old slave hymn in her head thinking to herself. What has become of our people? What has America done to the sons and daughters of Africa? Oh my people the suffering of your ancestors runs deep within your blood. You still suffer. You suffer from post traumatic stress that has been passed down from generation to generation caused by the evil, sadistic, dehumanizing institution of slavery. You're crying out for help. Your rebelling against a system created to keep you down in the belly of destitution and poverty. The disease of ignorance has reached the pupils of your mind so you run blindly through America's ghettos hating and killing this country to its knees and on its knee it will beg and plea for your forgiveness. Forgive them you will, cause the compassionate nature of the African still swims in your blood stream. Deidre could have sworn she saw a tear run down the dark wrinkled skin of Miss Evelyn.

Three days after that incident had Web running for his life. Deidre was getting off the train at the 105th street train station. As she came out of the stairwell of the subway, she could hear footsteps running towards her from the empty lot in front of the station. Then she heard it Boc! Boc! Boc! Boc! She froze in fear and she saw someone fall face down to the ground. It was nighttime so she couldn't get a good look at his face. Then she recognized Web emerge from the lot standing over the wounded person.

"Bitch nigga wassup now!" Web barked pointing a black handgun down at the guy who was now crying and pleading.

"I'm sorry man I swear. I'll pay you, just don't kill me. The bitch ain't worth it. I'll give you what you want!"

"Let me see your face!" Web ordered the wounded man while kicking him on his rear end causing him to wince in agonizing pain. Painfully he rolled over looking up at Web with a pleading, fearful expression.

"Web I'm hurt man. I can't feel my legs, don't do this!" His pleas were cut short when Web squeezed the trigger. Deidre let out a low scream as she witnessed the atrocity that forever silenced the man. To Deidre a silence that swallowed her in it. She heard nothing, not even the L train leaving the station. Web looked over at Deidre. His stare was scary and blank. Surprisingly he smiled at Deidre and then suddenly he jogged off into the Canarsie night. Growing up in the projects, Deidre's street education taught her that minding your business and being tight lipped was the key to surviving in the urban jungle. Web knew that she understood that fact. The shooting was a secret shared between Deidre and Web; a story that Deidre would never tell to anyone.

Two and a half years after that dreadful day, Web was arrested for another murder he committed on the far side of the projects. When Deidre read about it in The Canarsie Courier, the local paper, she sat on the project bench with Liz deep into the article. Then something in the article jumped out at Deidre. Words that sent her memory back to a place it didn't want to revisit.

"Webster Daniels is also a suspect in the 1994 slaying of Raheem Caldwell of Canarsie who was found shot at the 105th street station. Police say that murder was allegedly the result of an extortion plot formulated by Daniels that turned deadly. Daniels allegedly videotaped himself and the girlfriend of Caldwell in a sexual encounter. Daniels allegedly blackmailed Caldwell's girlfriend to aid him in orchestrating the robbery of Caldwell for money and drugs.

"Daniels became the primary suspect when the girlfriend of Caldwell informed Caldwell of Daniels intentions. Authorities received information from sources that say Caldwell attempted to go after

Daniels seeking revenge but didn't get a chance. Instead, Daniels allegedly got to Caldwell first. Police have yet to make a case against Daniels for the Caldwell murder. The girlfriend of Caldwell was found murdered a week after Caldwell's death. Daniels is a suspect in that homicide also. If you have any information on these murders..."

As Deidre lay on her bed half listening to Diondre carry on about why she withheld the story of the fight at the hair show. Deidre thought about that article she read about Web back in 96. A story of the extortion plot and the sex tape, it all seem strange to Deidre the similarities in the situation she's in with Jabbar. Is *there some type of connection?* She asked herself. *Why am I thinking that, those men don't know each other from Adam. Nah!* Jabbar is probably broke and desperate for some cash. He most likely messed up one of his client's money and couldn't come up with nothing else. He could have at least asked for help instead of this. Men and their silly pride. Still Deidre had to think of a way out of the mess she created without anyone getting hurt. She didn't think anyone would get hurt physically. Jabbar didn't appear as a man of violence she could tell he was a teddy bear under the machismo. The heartbreak and feelings of betrayal was what she wanted to avoid; that and the destruction of her reputation.

"Are you listening to me Dee. This has to be dealt with." Diondre ranted. Suddenly Deidre felt herself about to vomit. She jumped up quickly and sprinted to the bathroom "You need to see a doctor,"

Diondre uttered entering the bathroom watching as Deidre vomited in the toilet.

"I think you're right," Deidre said wiping her mouth with the back of her hand. Her eyes watered and Diondre noticed the puffiness under them. She looked like she hasn't slept in days.

Diondre didn't know she hasn't been able to get a good sleep since her act of infidelity.

At a private doctors office in Crown Heights, Deidre sat in the waiting area nervously waiting for the results of several test she took, she secretly prayed she had no disease, especially an STD or some other contagious one like TB or something that wouldn't go away like Hepatitis.

She thought that maybe it was the flu or a stomach virus that she may have caught in Virginia. After about two hours of waiting the African doctor that's been dealing with Diondre's family for years came out. His smile sent a message that whatever it was wasn't that serious. Deidre was still nervous. "Deidre..." the doctor announce in his African accent. "Honey you are pregnant."

"Yes!" Diondre jumped out of his seat yelling.

"Thank you God!" Deidre sat in the chair with a pale face stunned by the news. She didn't know if she should be happy or sad. Her only thought were, *oh my God what if I'm pregnant by Jabbar? Please God don't punish me like that. Please!*

"We're having a baby Dee. Do you hear that a baby!" Diondre hugged Deidre. Deidre pretended that everything was okay. She hugged Diondre tightly and put her mouth to his ear.

"Thank you Dre. Thank you for making me your woman. I love you.

Chapter 5

Debby

Debby sat in the employees lounge after putting on her uniform consisting of a white button down shirt, a black knee length skirt and the apron she wore over it. She wanted to smoke a cigarette before starting her day. As she smoked she was, acting as if she were interested in the conversation that three Richmond girls were trying desperately to get her fully involved in.

"Size don't matter it's the bank account that does," one of the girls said. Debby looked at them thinking to herself *these country bitches are the dumbest chicks I've ever been around. Their hairdos are whack, they can't dress and they fuck with the corniest niggas I ever seen. These niggas is all wannabe ballers and rappers.*

"You from New York. Let me ask you this. If Jay-Z had a little dick would that stop you from fucking him?" One of the girls that had a finger-wave hairstyle asked Debby. Debby blew out smoke and just shrugged her shoulders. Then another of the girls asked the irritating question a lot of people out of New York ask New Yorkers when they meet them.

"Do you see Lil Kim? What about Fabulous, he is so cute?"

Debby walked out of the lounge to start her day. When she entered the dining area, she heard the voice of the owner call out to her. "Miss Clarkson can I have a word with you in my office?" the heavy set, pudgy faced that reminded Debby of Boss Hog from the TV show Dukes of Hazard requested.

"Have a seat Miss Clarkson," Boss hog pointed to a chair he had positioned a foot away from his large oak wood desk filled with pictures of family members and a computer that he sat at most of the day. Rumor was he sat in his office surfing on internet porn sites masturbating to them.

He paced behind his desk not looking Debby in her face. "Miss Clarkson it's been brought to my attention through a thorough background check that you lied on your application for employment about your criminal history."

Debby sighed shaking her head. She knew this day was coming. She didn't think so soon though. It's been a month and she needed more time to save up some money. That way she could put Ty-Ran in private school like he was in New York.

What Debby didn't know was that word got around about her scuffle at the hair show.

This wasn't New York. Word traveled around small cities like Richmond quicker than a New York minute. When the boss heard of the scuffle and found out that Debby was really from New York instead of Richmond like she put on the application he did some digging.

"A thief? Oh hell naw she's got to go." He told one of his supervisors. "I knew that accent wasn't Southern. I can't believe I fell for those lies."

Debby tried to explain that she put all that behind her and that it was her way of surviving in an expensive city like New York.

"I moved down here to get away from that life sir. All I need is a chance to prove that," Debby pleaded but her pleas fell on deaf ears.

"Miss Clarkson, I can't have a former thief or any type of thief at my establishment. I'm sorry but you have to go. Here's your pay for the week," he handed her a hundred dollar check.

Debby drove Web's jeep that he let her borrow while he slept at her apartment back home. She stopped at a grocery store to buy food for the house. Debby was happy that little Ty-Ran got along with Web. It helped with little Ty-Ran fragile emotions in coping with the loss of his father.

Debby stopped at a Wal-Mart to pick up Ty-Ran a new game for his brand new Playstation 3. At first Debby thought about resorting to her old ways and stealing as much as she could from Wal-Mart but she changed her mind and only stole one item. A pack of magnum condoms for Web's big dick self, she thought to herself. She smiled at the old feelings that being a thief gave her. The rush excited her. It even made her horny.

Debby with grocery bags in her hands opened the door to her apartment courtesy of the N.Y.P.D's $20,000 check. They gave it to her as a payment on a house but Debby's Brooklyn mentality had her pocket half the money, spend the other half on furnishing the apartment that she got through public assistance. She moved into Richmond's south-side projects right next to the club where the hair show was held.

Debby heard music blasting from in the apartment and she could smell the distinct odor of marijuana coming from the place. When she opened the door, it was as if Beyonce was in the house having a concert on her living room floor. "Damn Web turn that shit down nigga!" Debby yelled over the music. The first thing she did was checked her son's room. Her heart begin to pound as she saw a rope tied on the door handle of her son's room that ran up the apartment hall where the other end was tied to the bathroom door. "Ty-Ran!" Debby yelled while untying the rope.

"Mommy, get me outta here please!" Ty-Ran yelled from behind the door. Beyonce's voice muffled his cries. Debby got the rope untied and open the door hugging her son who had tears running down his face. She checked to see if he was hurt and was put at ease when he wasn't.

"Go wait next door at Keisha's house. I'll be there in a minute,"

"But Mommy..."

"Go Ty-Ran now!" Debby barked. Ty-Ran ran out of the house quickly. Debby grabbed a steak knife and walked to her bedroom door that was closed. She put her ear to the door and could hear the bed squeaking and grunts. With one hard swift kick Debby sent the door crashing in. what she saw next was something out of a bizarre movie.

Something she thought she would never personally experience, a nightmare. With sweat dripping down his black naked body there was Web pumping his swollen eleven inches in the ass of a light-skinned man wearing a leather mask on his face.

"Oh shit you faggot mufucka. What the fuck are you doing?" Debby roared. The masked man jumped up, grabbed his clothes off the floor and ran out the room. When he ran pass Debby she swung the knife at him slicing his arm. He yelped in pain as blood squirted on the wall.

"Get yo faggot ass outta here! Web who is that? Matter fact fuck who he is, get yo faggot ass out!" Debby pointed the knife at Web.

Web was putting his clothes on looking at Debby embarrassed. "Deb hold up ma. Listen it ain't what it seems like. Yo I got a plan..."

"Web shut yo lying faggot ass up! A plan? Nigga please. What's yo plan, fuck him in the ass then rob his house? Right Web! I been heard you was a faggot but my blind dumb ass gave you the benefit of the doubt. Why? I don't know. I done lost a lot fucking with you. A lot of good people stop fucking with me cause of yo faggot ass. I'm done, Web get yo ass out of my life for good!"

"Deb you don't mean that baby." Web pleaded trying to reach out to Debby. She pulled back and held the knife up ready to strike.

"Web don't fucking touch me. I swear on my son and you going tie my son's door locking him in? You lucky I don't call the cops on yo ass!"

"I didn't want him to run off while I was putting my plan together," Web said.

"You faggot I swear get out!" Debby yelled. She watched as Web's face became menacing.

"Yo all that faggot shit. You going chill out fa real Deb I'm telling you," Web threatened.

"Oh what you going to do Web, shoot me? You already ruined my life so killing me would only help nigga. Who else did you kill, my son's father, Cornbread? Go head Web get yo gun. You gangsta right? Big bad Web! You ain't nothing but a faggot," Deb taunted.

Web was ready to punch her but seeing her son and a few neighbors standing at the door made him change his mind. He just walked out of the house jumped in his jeep and drove off. All Debby could do was fall to the floor and sob.

That night Debby sat on her bed with tears in her eyes holding a bottle of pain pills she removed from her nightstand. It felt like the world was against her. She felt like something was out to ruin her life. Nothing could go right. Debby didn't want her messed up life to affect her son's life so she thought that maybe if she was gone that he would be placed in a home that would be beneficial to his upbringing. She smiled as the tears still flow thinking back to the day she gave birth to her seven pound five ounce baby boy.

It was the happiest day of her life. Even big Ty-Ran was there holding her hand as she pushed her whole reason for living into this world. The smile left her face when she thought about the world she has bought her baby into.

"I'm so sorry baby," she cried while slowly

opening the bottle of pills. Debby jumped and quickly put the pills back in the nightstand as she heard her bedroom door open and the voice of her son called out.

"Mommy?"

"Yes baby what's wrong?" Debby asked turning the light on that sat on her nightstand.

"I can't sleep in my room. Can I sleep with you?" Ty-Ran asked with a sad voice dressed in a two-piece Polo pajama suit.

"Of course baby come here," Debby said pulling her blanket back as Ty-Ran hopped in the bed. She held him close to her chest listening to him breathe. Right then and there she decided it was worth living. She couldn't see herself anywhere without her son. Even in death.

Chapter 6

Liz

"Surprise!" Liz was shocked after walking into the salon to a surprise party, courtesy of Deidre.

"Happy Birthday Liz!" Deidre walked towards Liz with a gift wrapped in her hand. Liz was at a loss for words as other employees and customers wished her happy birthdays and gave her gifts. Liz unwrapped Deidre's gift and hugged Deidre thanking her for the lingerie. Diondre hugged her and handed her a gift she always said she wanted an iPod. Liz's face lit up when she saw the iPod. "Oh God Dre thank you so much. It is on and popping!"

Physically Liz healed from the fight she had with Debby, well somewhat. The swelling of her face and lips were gone. The only visible remnant of the scuffle was a bruise under her eye that she covered with her Dolce and Gabbana shades. Mentally Liz was still hurt by the ordeal.

At first, she was extremely angry with Debby wanting nothing but sweet revenge, but as she contemplating the whole situation alone for one week, she began to feel guilt.

The initial guilt was from her being the transgressor in the whole physical confrontation. She told herself, *I should have never slapped Debby.* Even more idiotic was her turning her back afterwards. Liz grew up with Debby and knew better than to hit her and not expect a fight.

Debby fought all her life and mostly with men, and fighting men hardened Debby and turned her into a force to be reckon with so it was nothing for her to fight a woman. That was a walk in the park to Debby.

Another thing Liz felt bad about is not being more understanding in Debby's situation. Debby has a hard time being alone. Ever since Liz knew Debby, Debby always had a man in her life. Either a man she was just having sex with or a man she was feeling emotionally. She was emotionally attached to Ty-Ran but the way he treated her made her run to other men for comfort, so when Web came home it was like he filled a void in Debby's life. Debby was a tough girl but at the same time emotionally vulnerable and gullible. All it took was for a man to give Debby mind-blowing sex and a couple of dollars and Debby was hooked. Is it Debby's fault that women, especially black women growing up in single parent homes in the ghettos of America get the wrong impression to what the love of a man is suppose to be like?

Many of these women see their mothers emotionally abused as well as physically by their fathers or by men their mothers love. These mothers accept the abuse because they feel that there isn't a man that will treat them any better. They mistake the abuse as a show of love. That is a Stockholm syndrome. A syndrome is where victims of the abuse blame themselves. Liz felt she should have heard Debby out before overreacting. After receiving hugs and welcome back greeting throughout the salon, Liz pulled Deidre into the back office.

"Liz wassup girl?" Deidre asked walking to the desk acting as if she were looking for something when in reality she was nervous about why Liz wanted to talk to her alone.

"Dee I haven't seen Jabbar all week. I can't get through to him on the phone he hasn't been at his house. I'm worried Dee I miss him," Liz said sounding like a wounded puppy. Deidre exhaled then unintentionally smiled.

"Why are you smiling...?" Liz paused looking around the office then walking over to the office bathroom looking in "Is he here, is that another surprise?" Liz asked excitedly.

"No, no Liz. I was smiling because I'm just happy to see you back to normal. You're no longer bitter over the V.A thing." Deidre lied. Lying to Liz and Diondre made Deidre feel sick.

She wanted so badly to let it out. The guilt was eating away at her but how do you tell your fiancé a man you're been with since high school who treats you like you're the mother of God, and your best friend that you grew up with and been through so many ups and downs, a horrible secret like the one Deidre held. Deidre told herself that soon it would be all over with and they could continue with their lives. As soon as she did what Jabbar asked she could breathe again.

"Yeah the VA thang. I wanted to talk to you

about that too," Liz said as if she were about to reveal bad news. Liz relayed her guilty feeling to Deidre about the whole thing. Deidre nodded her head as Liz talked. Deidre heard Liz explanation but was in her own thoughts about what lay ahead for her.

"In due time these wounds will heal and those guilty feeling will be gone," Deidre said to Liz but really saying the words to herself.

Liz and Deidre return into the front of the salon where the festivities continued. Music played as Liz's cake was placed in the middle of the shop. A giant size candle shaped as the number 33 sat on top of the cake. Diondre put his arm around Liz shoulder as she walked to the cake.

"Where's Jabbar? I haven't seen him all week." Diondre mumbled to Liz. A sad feeling came over Liz at Jabbar not being there but she didn't want to ruin the party her best friend, put together for her. Diondre and Deidre were in her life before Jabbar and would be thereafter.

"I don't know where he is but the cake damn sure look good!" Liz said excitedly. Then everyone begin singing the happy birthday lullaby. "Happy Birthday to you, happy birthday dear Liz...!"

When Diondre and Deidre got home that night, Diondre, seeing that Deidre's bout with sickness was over, set up a romantic evening. He had candles lit and rose's pedals on the floor leading to their king-size bed. Diondre always heard that a woman's sex felt better when they were pregnant, he wanted to test that myth. Deidre was more than happy to please her man after a few weeks of holding back. If only Diondre knew the real reason.

They soaked in a candle lit bubble bath together drinking champagne. Deidre stroked Diondre's organ while she leaned on his chest. He in turn reached over her waist and let his fingers massage her clit. She moaned and arched her back as Diondre kissed the back of her neck and nibbled on her ear. Even in the hot water her skin goose bumped from the feeling. Her ears were her spot.

Deidre stood up and looked back at Diondre with her arms outstretch towards him.

"C'mon baby I need you in me now."

Diondre quickly jumped up splashing bubbles and water on the bathroom floor. His manhood was stiff as a log and he couldn't wait to get him some. He carried her into the bedroom and laid her down on her back kissing her as he eased her on to the sheets, to Diondre's amazement, Deidre took control. She pushed Diondre off her and seductively mumbled, "Lay down baby I got this."

"Okay baby as you wish," Diondre surrendered playfully.

"I'm gonna go set the alarm don't you go nowhere," Deidre commanded getting up while Diondre admired her naked body. Her plump butt cheeks jiggled as she walked out of the room. Deidre went to the key pad next to their door and pressed a code on their ADT alarm system.

She jogged back into the room and hopped on the bed immediately sitting on top of Diondre. She reached over in her nightstand and pulled out a small bottle of massage oil that she poured into her hands and began rubbing them together. She rubbed the warm oil now warm from the friction caused by her rubbing hands and massage Diondre's chest and stomach. He moaned in anticipation of her hands massaging the rest of his body. He almost lost his breath when her hands reached his erection.

"Oh my God baby that feels good," he moaned as she stroked his hardness with one hand and with the other hand, she gently played with his balls.

"You like it baby? I love you Diondre," Deidre said in a soft seductive voice Diondre closed his eyes and mumbled. "I love you too. Baby don't stop what you're doing."

"Ssh. I got something better," Deidre said. Diondre could feel her move while still massaging him. Then he felt her tongue tease the tip of his pole. He grabbed the sheets in a tight grip as Deidre glided her mouth down the length of his shaft. She moaned as she blessed her man with an oral delight.

"I want you to taste me while I taste you," Deidre mumbled getting into the sixty-nine position. When she put her pretty pussy in his face, he could see it glistening from her own juices. He quickly delved in and returned the favor. Deidre moaned while moving her waist in a round about making her juices cover Diondre's face.

The feeling she was giving Diondre made his concentration to performing on her difficult. It felt so good he sometimes had to hold his breath. Then he felt his balls about to release its load.

"Baby I'm bout to cum. Oh god!" Diondre grunted. Deidre begin to suck with more aggression stroking at the same time.

"I want you in my mouth baby," she moaned and as Diondre's body begins to release his load she let the warm liquid slam into her throat and swallowed every drop. She continued to suck even after he came. She turned to face him still straddling him bending over so her face could meet his. They begin to kiss passionately. She could taste her juices on his mouth. She reached behind her massaging his limp dick back to a bulging erection. Once she felt he was ready, she placed him inside her.

Diondre held her waist as she began to ride him. She played with her own nipples biting her bottom lip with her eyes closed. Diondre palmed her soft rear and squeezed them spreading them apart.

"Oh Dre, oh baby you feel so good. Don't stop baby fuck me!" Deidre panted placing her hands on Diondre's chest speeding up her thrust. The slapping of her cheeks against his upper thighs echoed through the room. Diondre turned her around and pulled her legs off the bed he stood up and hit it from behind.

"Dre! Dre! Oh yes baby. Ooooh yeeeah!" Deidre screamed feeling herself being filled by his largeness. After five minutes in that position Dre turned her on her back and pushed her legs all the way back making her knees touch the bed. From that position, he went in her in a slow motion making his hips move in a roundabout motion touching every part of her insides. Deidre gripped the sheets almost pulling them off the bed. With her eyes closed tight she squealed, "ooh Dre, oh baby I'm yours. Baby, oh baby pleeease don't stop! Oh god I'm cummiiin Dre!"

Dre watched as his shaft became drenched in her creamy wetness. He bit his bottom lip as he felt himself about to give up the baby making fluid the male body produced.

"AAAAH, oh shit yes!" He grunted as his cream entered into Deidre's cave. He collapsed on top of her, both of them out of breath. He looked into her face and kissed her lips. "I'm so in love with you, Deidre."

Deidre smiled at him saying. "And I'm too in love with you Diondre."

Afterwards Diondre fell asleep while Deidre laid there in deep thought. Eventually she fell asleep.

Not long after, Diondre thought he heard whispering in the room. He reached behind him feeling for Deidre. She wasn't in bed. Then someone cut the light on temporarily blinding Diondre who closed his eyes then opened them slowly to get a better view. When his vision cleared his heart almost leaped out of his chest once he saw a masked man with his arms around Deidre's neck with a pistol to her temple.

"Diondre do as they say honey. Give them want they want!" Deidre cried.

"Take it easy man. Listen she's pregnant don't hurt her." Diondre said putting his hands up standing up slowly. Then another masked man walked into the bedroom carrying a Mac-11 machine gun. He walked over to Diondre and without saying a word rammed the pistol onto Diondre's head knocking him to the floor opening a four inch gash on his forehead.

"Oh God please don't hurt him. You said you wouldn't hurt him!" Deidre yelled.

Diondre's vision blurred and his head was spinning but he wondered why Deidre say, "You said you wouldn't hurt him." When did they say that? How long have they been in the house? And how did they get pass the alarm? These were all the questions that ran through Diondre's mind as he crawled on the floor blood pouring down his face.

"Nigga what the fuck you looking at? Get yo ass into the living room!" the masked man kicked Diondre in his ribs. Diondre grunted in pain feeling his rib crack. Diondre stood up and led the men into the living room. Diondre looked at Deidre frightened face as blood dripped on the expensive area rug.

"I don't have any money man. Not here," Diondre said holding his cracked ribs. CRACK!

The blow from the gun crashed into Diondre's face knocking him to the floor. "Listen to this homeboy. If you want to live to see this baby that your girl is carrying born, you're not gonna tell me there's no money in here. What you're gonna do is get the money," The masked man growled bending over with his face close to Diondre's. Diondre could smell liquor through the mask.

"You know what, this nigga think this is a joke. Maybe if we take oh girl here into the room and sample her goodies, maybe this nigga will see this ain't a game. You go first son." The guy standing over Diondre said to his partner holding Deidre at gunpoint.

"Yo! Yo! Hold up man, don't do this man. Leave her out of this please!" Diondre pleaded.

"All you gotta do is open the safe give us what we want and we walk out of here. You go back to your Huxtable life and that's that." The gunman said.

Diondre stood up, and somewhat dizzy walked over to the painting of Elijah Muhammad and took it off the wall exposing his built in safe.

"Okay baby that's what I'm talking bout. That must be some good pussy your girl got.

This nigga jumped up when I was talkin' bout giving her some," the gunman joked.

Diondre slowly turn the dial on the safe tryna clear his head of the dizzy feeling he was experiencing. More questions popped in his head. *How did they know that I had a safe? I'm being set up, but by who? Who are these men?*

"I ain't got all day my man lets hurry it up cause your girl is one pretty bitch and if I look at her one more time my dick gonna get hard."

Diondre opened the safe revealing its contents. There were papers neatly piled in yellow folders next to stacks of crispy one hundred dollar bills in piles of a thousand dollars. All together the safe contained closed to 90,000 in cash.

In a quick flash Diondre felt a blow on his

head then everything went blank. "Nooo!"

Deidre yelled. "You didn't have to hit him like that. He opened the safe!" As Diondre laid unconscious Deidre looked at the one of the men with a menacing stare. "Jabbar this wasn't part of the plan. You said you would take the money and leave. Why are you doing this?"

Jabbar lifted his mask revealing his face to her. He looked over at his partner who was loading the money in the bag. "C'mon baby lets go..." Jabbar said, then looked at Deidre and smiled.

"He'll be aiight for ya'll's wedding."

With the money in the bag Jabbar and his partner quickly left the brownstone. Deidre crawled over to Diondre shaking him awake. Diondre was unresponsive. Deidre ran into the kitchen and dialed 911.

"911 please send someone over now. Some guys just broke in my house robbed us and knocked my husband unconscious. Please hurry!"

***

When Liz got home that night she stopped at the mailbox in the hallway of her building to pick up her mail. She realized that she hadn't picked her mail up in a week stressing over Jabbar's absence and the Debby situation. She quickly brushed through the mail from bill collectors, phone company, credit card applications and other junk mail until she saw a envelop with Debby's name on it. Liz rushed up to the apartment so she could read Debby's letter.

Dear Liz,

First I would like to say that I really need you to read this please. If you decide that after reading this letter that you cannot forgive me I will understand. You have all the reason in the world to be mad at me forever but I know your heart Liz and I can't see you being like that so with that being said, I want to sincerely apologize for everything that happened. You were right about everything Liz. Web isn't the man for me, nor is he the man I thought he was. I found out that Web is gay. I found out the hard way by finding him in my bed with another man. While I was at work, he had the nerve to lock my son in the room while he was in my bed fucking some dude with a mask on his face. Anyway he's gone out of my life forever. I miss our friendship badly Liz, there is no friend in the world like you. Oh god Liz I need so bad for you to forgive me. I need so bad to hug my best friend and tell you in your face that I'm sorry. My son needs his aunt Lizzy. I have no one else Liz. I'm so lonely down here and this country shit ain't me. I should have never gave up my apartment in New York so when I come back I have to start over. I just wanna come back knowing that I've been forgiven for what I did to you and that we can forever remain friends

Love your friend
Debby

While reading the letter Liz laughed at some of Debby's word and when the letter was over Liz cried. She too missed their friendship. Liz was happy she received the letter from Debby because she wanted to say the same thing. Liz was shocked about the Web being gay thing.

"Drama! Drama! Drama!" was all Liz could say.

Liz showered before lying on her couch to watch TV. She tried again to get in contact with Jabbar. All she got was his voice mail.

"Where is he? God!" she said frustrated. Liz sucked her teeth while walking into her bedroom looking into her closet. Once she found what she was looking for she stared at it and sighed. "And I was about to throw you away." Liz sat back on the couch, turned on her gadget, and placed it between her legs. "Ooh Yes!"

BROOKLYN SEXY PART 2

Chapter 7

Diondre

Brooklyn Federal Courthouse

A week later

"Mister Gaston can you tell this Grand Jury what took place on the date mentioned on the police report involving you and Mister Bennet?" the U.S. attorney for the Southern District of New York asked as he paced in front of the witness stand Gaston adjusted his black tie that he wore with his black suit. Gone were the baggy jeans and other urban clothing he wore as he drove around in his Dodge Magnum committing various crimes across the country. Now he looked like a man on his way to Sunday school. Gaston looked at the jury in the large empty courtroom. The proceeding was closed to the public, and a defense attorney isn't allowed to participate in a Grand jury hearing, and begin his testimony.

"Yes Sir. Me and James Benet..."

The U.S. attorney interrupted Gaston asking, "For the record what name do you know Mister Bennet by. What is his alias?"

"I know him as Gray. He's called that cause the color of his eyes. He also calls himself Jabbar."

"Thank you Mister Gaston you may continue."

"Yeah so, me and Gray we go up to the Bronx..."

Back in the Present

The next morning Deidre sat crying in a chair next to Diondre's hospital bed as he lay unconscious with tubes connected to almost every part of his body. The blow to his head fractured his skull causing trauma to his brain. Diondre was in a coma. Deidre could hear Liz voice in the hall asking a nurse the where about of Diondre Taylor.

How did she find out? Deidre thought to herself. *Oh god this is the last thing I wanted, for everyone to know about this mess I done got myself and Diondre in.*

"Dee. Oh god Dee what happened?" Liz said walking into the room covering her mouth as she looked at Diondre laying there helpless. Deidre almost wet her pants when she looked behind Liz and saw Jabbar come walking in the room with a confused and concern expression on his face.

"Oh my god Deidre what happened. Who did this mess?" Jabbar asked really putting on an Oscar winning performance. Deidre glared at him with a murderous expression then she quickly looked at Diondre. Deidre knew exactly what Jabbar was doing. He was there to see what information the cops got. Deidre also knew that she had to play into his act in order not to expose herself. She was just as guilty as Jabbar was.

"We don't know, they wore mask," Deidre said wiping tears from her face with a napkin as she looked pitifully as Diondre. The sound of the heart monitor made Deidre more depressed.

Liz hugged her best friend and tears begin to fall down her face also.

"I'm gonna run and get something to drink. You want anything?" Liz asked Deidre as she stood up to exit the room. "You baby?" she asked Jabbar, after Deidre shook her head.

"Nah I'm good. Go on I'll wait here," Jabbar replied.

When Liz was a distance, away Jabbar pulled up a chair and sat in front of Deidre.

Between clenched teeth Deidre said, "You played yourself. You didn't have to do this. I told you 1 wasn't gonna co-sign you beating him and you gave me your word."

Jabbar sat back in a nonchalant manner. "What did the cops find out?"

Tears ran down Deidre's face as she answered.

"Nothing. You have no worries. You got what you want now get out of our lives and Liz too. You don't love her you used her to get close to us. Tell me this though Jabbar. How did you find out about us? What made you pick us?"

Jabbar leaned closer to Deidre with a grin on his face replying. "I didn't look for ya'll. Ya'll found me."

"Hey Dee I think some police are here to talk

to you. They're at the nurse's station asking about Diondre," Liz said returning to the room carrying a can of Red Bull. Just as Liz finished mentioning that, the cops came in two suit and tie wearing white men.

"Mrs. Taylor?" one of the detectives said looking between Deidre and Liz. Deidre didn't bother to correct them, plus she hoped after this mess blew over that she would be Mrs. Diondre Taylor.

"Yes that's me." Deidre said watching as Jabbar stood up to stand against the wall so the detective could get closer to Deidre.

"Mrs. Taylor my name is detective Garoener and this is my partner detective Chamberlain. We're from robbery-homicide division. I need to ask you a few questions."

"We'll step out for a minute Dee okay." Liz said grabbing Jabbar's hand. The detective named Chamberlain who stood by the door gave Jabbar a look of skepticism. A look of trying to recognize a familiar face. Jabbar didn't notice the cop's glare.

"Mrs. Taylor you gave an| initial statement to the detectives on the scene. I noticed in that statement you said you set the alarm at around midnight is that correct?" the detective asked holding a pen and a pad in his hand as he sat next to Deidre.

"It was around that time, I'm pretty sure," Deidre answered. The detective writing in the pad looked up at his partner who shrugged his shoulders.

"Mrs. Taylor, crime scene investigators found

out that the alarm was never set that night. So could you be mistaken? You know we just need to clarify some things." The detective noticed the blood rush to Deidre's face after he made his statement.

"Do you expect me to be sure about everything that happened? All I know is we came home, made love and next thing you know guns are being pointed at us and my husband is beaten almost to death. I usually set the alarm every night maybe that night after coming from a party drinking and all that I forgot. Deidre said irritated.

The detective looked down at his pad. "One more question then we'll be on our way...."

Deidre folded her arm across her chest and gave the detective a look as if he were being bothersome. Being a veteran detective, Deidre's actions made him suspicious. Why would a woman whose husband and house has been invaded and robbed be angry at investigators trying to bring the people responsible for it to justice?

Was she hiding something? The detective wasn't a psychologist or an expert in human behavior, and people react differently in certain situations, but his suspicions usually turned out to be correct. He wasn't a gambling man but he was willing to bet she knew more than she was letting on.

"Do you have a relative that you may have had a fallen out with or is on drugs that may have wanted to do something to you or your husband as a payback?" the detective inquired.

"No!" Deidre barked. "What type of question

is that? What you think all black people have druggies in their families? I resent that question detective."

"What about your husband?" the detective said calmly. Deidre face became even more flustered. "No. Hell no damnit. What does this have to do with what happened?"

"There was no forced entry. So either the door was open or somebody had the key. This is Brooklyn ma'am I don't think people leave their doors open."

As the detectives got up to leave, Liz walked in with Jabbar in tow. "Dee you aiight?

What's wrong?" Liz asked wondering why she heard Deidre yelling and why she looked pissed off.

"Yeah I'm ok." Deidre answered trying to calm herself down. She couldn't believe the audacity of these cops. Drug addicts or enemies in family always with the stereotypes.

"Sir, can I ask you what your name is?" Deidre heard one of the detectives asked noticing the question being directed to Jabbar.

Jabbar looked nervous as he answered. "Jabbar, is there a problem officer?"

"What is your last name sir?" Detective Chamberlain asked.

Jabbar was thinking. *What are these crackers up to? I don't have warrants, I just saw my P. O. two weeks ago so if I had a warrant he would of knew and I would have got locked up at the parole office. They got me mixed up.* "Bennet."

The detectives smiled at each other before

they reached for their handcuffs. "A.K.A Gray correct?

Turn around and face the door. Don't do anything that will turn this into an ugly situation Gray."

The detective name Chamberlain ordered.

"Gray? My name ain't Gray. I told ya'll my name. What am I under arrest for?" Jabbar asked as they cuffed and searched him.

"You're wanted by the FBI. A grand jury indicted you a week ago. There's been a warrant out since." Chamberlain the larger of the two detectives said.

"Hold up ya'll got the wrong person. He didn't do nothing!" Liz yelled trying to step between the detectives and Jabbar. Deidre quickly pulled Liz away.

"Ma'am please stay back or we will be force to restrain you and place you under arrest for obstruction of justice," the detective warned Liz.

"Jabbar what are they talking about? Why do the F.B.I, want you?" Liz cried to Jabbar.

As they led Jabbar out the room walking him toward the exit, he turned to face Liz.

"Baby don't cry, I ain't do nothing This is a mistake. It will be straightened out by my lawyer. I'll be out tonight."

"Call me so I can come down to wherever you at. I promise!" Liz yelled to Jabbar as they placed him in the back of their unmarked black Crown Victoria.

Jabbar looked at Liz from the back window

and mouthed to a crying Liz. "I love you."

Liz leaned into Deidre's arms crying. Deidre all the while thinking *good ridden you bastard.*

A week later Jabbar was still locked up in the metropolitan Correctional Center in Manhattan with no bail, charged under the RICO Statute. The crimes alleged in the indictment were that Jabbar was part of a burglary ring that committed burglaries up and down the eastern seaboard of very expensive homes owned by very rich people, stealing over five million dollars worth of jewelry. It was alleged that Jabbar conspired to commit these acts with Lamar Gaston and a Cornelius Cornbread Collins. The most serious charge in the indictment was the murder of Cornbread to which Jabbar was named the killer.

***

Lamar Gaston sat in his cell at the Federal detention center in Philadelphia reading a letter that was sent from his mother's address in the Bronx. His mother or his little brother that lived there didn't write the letter.

Gas,

What up baby boy? You know who this be playboy. Listen I heard the song on the radio that you talkin bout. It's a bad tune my man. I let your old earth and little man hear it and they don't like it either. I'm a turn to the station again and if I get a shout out by D.J then the fat lady sings ya dig? And yo I could care less about twinkle toes, what's done is done. I just don't want to feature on the compilation or a lot of folks gonna wear hard bottoms.

– Edward Scissor Hands.

Gaston knew exactly what that letter meant. The song on the radio meant what he was telling the cops. The old earth and little man in the letter referred to his mother and little brother being in danger if he kept talking. Twinkle toes was in reference to Gaston's co-defendant Jabbar.

The writer was saying he didn't care about him ratting on Jabbar cause he don't know him or care about him just leave him out of it. Ed scissor hands was the name Web was called in Riker's Island. He was quick to cut a person up with razors or knives. Gaston knew the threat came from his former lover Web. When Web got a call from Gaston telling him about his arrest; Web immediately paid a visit to Gaston's mother home in the Kingsbridge section of the Bronx.

"Hey baby how you doing?" Gaston's seventy-year-old mother greeted Web at her door turning around to let Web in the house. She liked Web because he treated her like a mother and had good manners. She had no idea that Web was her son's gay lover and crime partner. The two men met on Riker's Island in 1997 before they were both sent to different prisons upstate New York. It was on

Riker's Island where Web came to terms with his own sexuality.

"Hey Miss Gaston how are you?" Web greeted the old woman.

"You want something to eat baby?" she asked Web.

"Naw I just stop by to give you some money for Lamar and I need you to address this letter to him for me," Web said handing her a sealed envelope and two-hundred dollars for Gaston's commissary.

"Okay baby I'll take care of that today."

Web hugged and kissed the old woman on her cheek before asking. "Where's little Jeff?"

"That boy running them streets somewhere with them other little knuckle heads he call friends."

"Tell him I said what's up." Web said. Web walked out of the house, stopped on the steps looking up and down the block where kids played and people stood in front of buildings chatting and hanging out. Web inhaled deeply then exhaled smiling.

Chapter 8

Liz

"What happen to your arm?"

"This? Playing ball in the gym," Jabbar replied covering a scar on his arm with his t-shirt as he and Liz sat at a table on the visiting floor of the M.C.C. This was Liz first visit to the prison since Jabbar was arraigned on the charges. Liz was still confused about the whole ordeal.

"Why'd you never tell me your name was James, what else haven't you told me Jabbar?"

Liz asked folding her arms across her chest with an angry expression on her face.

"Baby, James is my government name. I call myself Jabbar because I'm a conscious black man who has gave up the slave name," Jabbar answered. It was a reply that Liz knew so well. So many dudes in her neighborhood do not go by their birth names but rather be called by some name they came up with after learning some black history or becoming members of the five percenter's or Muslims but Liz still had other questions that needed to be clarified.

"What's this they saying you have a record and served time before? You never told me that?"

Jabbar's face showed his frustration at Liz cross-examination. "And if I did what would that have done for you Liz? Would it make you love me more or less? I'm tired of having to prove I'm a good person despite the fact I got arrested years back for burglary. I was young and dumb. I'm not proud of my past so I don't wear it as a badge like so many brothers do."

Jabbar words made Liz feel guilty. As if she were some type of saint who was prejudice to her own people that lived a struggling life trying to survive the best way they know how. She knew firsthand what that was like and she remembered being on the side of the visiting table Jabbar was on, only for a week for boosting but she knew. What she didn't know was that Jabbar was charged in the murder of Cornbread.

"I'm sorry baby I just don't like us holding secrets from each other. I told you everything there was to know about me," Liz said apologetically and in a tone of understanding. Jabbar held both of her hands in his. His touch was warm and Liz wanted so badly for them to be lying naked in bed together. She didn't get a chance to make love to him once he reappeared after his week of not being around.

The next morning Liz called Deidre to find out why the shop wasn't open, Deidre informed Liz of what happened and right before Liz left her apartment Jabbar popped up so they left for the hospital together.

"You right Liz. It's just that I tried to put those things behind me and move on."

Liz kissed Jabbar on his lips happy that Jabbar clarified the mystery of James Bennet. Liz playfully punched Jabbar's arm who winced from the pain. Liz mistakenly hit his recently wounded arm.

"Where were you that whole week? I was losing my mind trying to find out where you were. Don't do that to me," Liz said childishly.

"A friend of mines got locked up for tax evasion in Boston. I flew up there because I had some financial statements of his and he needed them. Plus, he needed to talk to me in person. I left my phone in the apartment rushing out," Jabbar concocted a good lie. When in all reality he was plotting the robbery of Diondre.

Even if Liz didn't believe him she convinced herself that he was telling her the truth. She loved Jabbar and all that mattered was that he loved her too.

"Baby I'm getting transferred out of here tomorrow," Jabbar said.

"Transferred? Where?" Liz asked with a worried expression. She knew that the Feds would ship prisoners anywhere in the country. She was afraid that they would ship Jabbar too far away from New York and she wouldn't be able to see him regularly. Her fears were confirmed when Jabbar answered, "Indiana." All Liz could do was stare at Jabbar as tears fell down her face.

"Hey baby welcome back," Deidre smiled holding on to Diondre's hands as he woke out of his coma. The three weeks he spent in a coma took a toll on his body. Diondre lost weight and his once shiny, smooth complexion had a dullness to it. Barely able to talk he smiled at Deidre.

Looking around he tried to familiarize himself with where he was at and how he got there. His memory was temporarily impaired due to the trauma and coma.

Deidre put her head close to his ears once she realized he was trying to talk.

"Where am I?" Diondre whispered.

Deidre kissed his hands as she held them between hers. "You're in Brooklyn Hospital baby."

"Why?" He asked in a whisper.

Deidre sighed before relaying the incident to Diondre, detailed without leaving one thing out. All Diondre did was shake his head in disbelief. The thoughts running through his mind was, *all I do is good by people and this is how life comes back at you? This is the exact reason why I don't believe in God. God wouldn't do this to a person that walks straight in a world filled with so much temptation and evil. If I were a believer in God, I would be considered one of the good righteous people. So what did I do to deserve this? Nothing. Nothing at all some low life dirt bag decided that he wanted to do wrong and he chose me. Why and how?* Those were the answers that Diondre needed and he wouldn't rest easy until he got them.

The next day, Diondre told Deidre to open the shop. He said there wasn't a reason why they should keep it closed until he got better when Deidre could open it and make money. Money that had to be made to pay bills cause the money they took was a hefty load that put a hurting on his pockets, Deidre walked in the shop from getting a cup of coffee to a conversation she knew would go on for hours.

Liz: "First off Oprah don't owe anybody an explanation of why she doesn't invite rappers like 50 cent or Snoop Dogg on her show. For the simple fact she represents the strong, independent woman who respects herself and why would she bring a man like Snoop on who showed up at an awards show with two black women on a leash and 50- cent calls himself a P-IM- P."

Female customer: "And she gives to good causes and charities that involve men and women so it's not like she's a sexist."

Male barber: "She should at least invite them on there and express that to them and maybe they'd agree."

Liz: "Please. All they'll do is sit there and come up with a justification of why they call women bitches and hoes talking bout some women are bitches and hoes and that's who their talking too. Why don't you try to uplift that woman who's behaving that way instead of putting her down?"

Male barber: "You got a hell of a point there I won't lie. At the same time what's the sense of inviting a child rapist, a racist or some other rascal when coming to the show won't change them?"

Liz and the other females got quiet on that point. The male barber who made the point received cheers and handshakes from the other males in the shop. Then Deidre made a comment.

"Farrakhan invited 50-cent on a show to squash a beef with Ja-Rule and he didn't show up. Snoop Dogg is married with children yet he shows up on a TV show that his children watch, with women on leashes. Is that how you want your son to view women? These guys make songs about killings and crime and their not saying don't do it, and they say their talking bout what's going on in the hood, why don't you talk about the solution also? Oprah is far from a sellout. She opened up a school in Africa for those girls. She shouldn't have to do that in this country where education is free and they build more prisons than schools. Why don't these rappers with their millions open up schools like Oprah did, tell me that? All they wanna do is come on Oprah to promote themselves. Yes there are women who exploit themselves, but if you aid her in doing it, you're just as guilty. Ask these rappers if their sister, mother or daughter decided to be a hoe would they support her or pimp her."

Male barber: "You didn't answer the thing about the bad people she will invite on her show?"

Deidre: "She is exposing the sickness to America, she's not supporting them. She is bringing a problematic issue to the forefront so our children can be safe."

The women in the salon applauded seeing that the men had no comeback to what Deidre said.

"On that note..." Deidre put a smile on her face and stood in the middle of the shop. "I have good news. Diondre is out of the coma and will be home in a few days."

"That's what's up! Ok Dre!" exclaimed a couple of barbers while others cheered and expressed their good feelings about the news.

Liz and Deidre looked at each other and simultaneously revealing their thoughts out loud.

"A party!"

Back at Diondre's hospital room. Diondre had a huge smile on his face as his parents and sisters walked in the room. He said to himself, at least something good came out of this I finally got my family together in New York.

Chapter 9

Debby

"Girl who's been doing your hair? This is a hot ghetto mess," Liz joked to Debby as she attached the store bought hair to Debby's real hair. They were listening to Keisha Cole's CD in Liz living room.

Debby couldn't be happier than to be back in good graces with her friend. Back in New York Debby and her son moved in with Big Ty-Ran's mother in the Red Hook projects until Debby was able to get an apartment.

"I had to go to them salons down there or my girlfriends from down there did it. I ain't no ghetto mess, shut up Liz," Debby remarked playfully.

"Liz wassup I'm going to spend tonight you with it?" Debby asked changing the hair subject. Ever since Jabbar got locked up Liz hadn't been going out. She stayed in the house after work waiting for Jabbar's long distance collect call that was very expensive. It didn't matter to Liz to her it was worth it. Hearing his voice put her at ease and was like foreplay for when she pulled out her toy.

"I ain't feeling the club thang like that Deb," Liz said in a depressing tone. Debby could identity with how Liz was feeling. Even though it didn't seem like it. Deb remembers when Web first got locked how the news made her depressed. Those first few days she didn't have an appetite, she sat around the house waiting for his calls, and when she did go out it was to run around running errands for him or running to Riker's Island to visit him. That lasted two months.

Then she met Ty-Ran. Thinking of how she met Ty-Ran made Debby sad that he was no longer around.

***

1997

"Deb you playing yourself sitting in the house all day cuz this nigga locked up. He wouldn't be like that if the shoe was on the other foot. Web fucks everything moving, don't act like you don't know," Debby listening to her boosting partner from Brownsville preach over the phone.

"I don't wanna hear his mouth about not being here for his call. This nigga be flippin."

Debby shot back. She was already frustrated at all the demands he made, so arguing with him was the last thing Debby wanted. It was draining. She was already losing weight.

"He's locked up for murder Deb. He ain't coming home no time soon. You ain't putting the pussy on lock for no ten to twenty years so you might as well get shit rolling now. There is gonna be some real live money getters at Sugar Hill. They throwing a memorial celebration for Biggie. Listen Deb you can't miss this."

"I ain't got nothing to wear and my hair ain't

done," Debby said sitting on her couch wearing a long Mickey mouse t-shirt with just a thong under it.

"You got that Puerto Rican chick that live on the other side of your projects that can do it and I just came back from downtown, I got some banging clothes for you. I'm coming over right now." The girl hung the phone up not giving Debby a chance to protest. Debby sighed hanging the phone up.

Five minutes after she hung up she got a call. When she answered she heard "please hold" from a computerized voiced. She knew it was Web.

"Debby?" Web said.

"Hey Web wassup boo?" Debby said happily. Her happy feeling quickly vanished when Web growled.

"Don't wassup me. I told you I need that money and I need you to bring that shit."

Debby couldn't believe the nerve of him. First, he wants her to be there for his calls but then he wants her to go get money to put on his books and bring him some weed. She wasn't doing the smuggling drugs up to no jail. It was far too risky. She'd rather steal out of a Fifth Avenue boutique with cameras than put some drugs in her pussy bringing it up to no jail. She knew plenty of chicks that got caught doing it and the niggas they did it for didn't even send one of their homies on the streets to bail the girl out. Hell no Debby told herself.

"How could I send you money when you want me to stay here for every call? Then you wanna be on the phone for two hours and I told you I'm not doing that other shit. Ask one of these other bitches you was fucking to do it." Debby growled back.

"People get real tough when a nigga locked up huh? You wouldn't talk like that if I was home. Now you mighty." Web snarled.

"That's the point Web, you're not here and you want me to do a hundred things I can't do. I'm stressed out too Web and you act like it's my fault you there," Debby whined.

Web was silent for almost two minutes. Debby thought he hung up until she heard him breathing. For jail, she wondered why she couldn't hear other inmates in the background.

"You know what Deb. I'm not going to fool myself thinking that your gonna be here for me if I get time. So I'ma fall back and let you decide what you wanna do." Debby heard a dial tone after Web said his piece.

"Oh no he didn't." Debby said looking at the phone as if it was a strange object. She hung up the phone and walked to her bedroom mumbling to herself. "This nigga just don't know, I'm a live my life not his. Fuck he think I am a slave? Fuck all that lying up in here waiting on his miserable ass. "I'm horny too. It is on."

That night as Debby and her girlfriend stood on a long line to get in the club on Dekalb Avenue, they dressed to impress, admired guys and girls who showed up dressed in the latest and flyest, hopping out of German engineers finest creations in car manufacturing also Japanese and American models too. The bass of some of the systems bumping out of the cars mixed in with the sound of the inside of the club. There were so many people outside waiting to get in the party almost started out there on the streets.

Once inside Debby and her friends danced with different men and drank shots of various drinks, courtesy of those men. One guy in particular caught Debby's full attention and she caught his. Debby wasn't the prettiest girl in the club but by far had the best body in there. Every man walked by either tried to talk to her or made comments as she walked by.

"Damn shorty that wagon you draggin' is happening..." One guy said and of course she heard the oldest one in the book. "Can I get fries with that shake?" even if the guy who said that line was cute, just cause he said that corny shit, she didn't waste her time.

But this one guy, she saw him smile at her every time she stole a look. She could tell he was a money getter. She knew there were guys who looked like they had money but were really broke. They would spent their last on an outfit and borrow a friend's car fronting like it was theirs. She knew those types. But what made it obvious that he was a boss type was the fact that he wasn't over dressed and jeweled.

When she walked over to the bar where he stood she noticed he wore a diamond flooded pinky ring and his watch a Swiss Movado with a diamond in the middle of the black face. He dressed nice but simple, a Izod short sleeve, a pair of polo jeans and tan Wallabee shoes.

What convinced Debby that he was an important guy was how people in the club acted when they approached him to speak. There were a few celebrity rappers and people in attendance that treated him like he was a celeb. Then there were street cats that acted as if they were paying homage to him. On one of those occasions, she heard his name. "Ran what up son? Bee sending a case of Cris over to you. He said a booth in VIP is ready for you."

"I guess you peeped me staring at you all night and wondering when I was going to stop acting like a pussy and approach you?" Ty-Ran said as he grabbed a seat next to Debby at the bar. Debby smiled at him noticing how white his teeth were and from how close he sat she could smell the Tom Ford cologne he was wearing.

"Something like that," Debby answered boldly.

"My name is Ty-Ran, and yours?" he asked offering his hand. Debby looked down at his manicured hand as if it were a foreign object. Then she extended her hand to his.

"Debby," she answered feeling the softness of his touch. She could tell he wasn't the type to get his hands dirty. He was a shot caller. Surprisingly Ty-Ran kissed the back of Debby's hand allowing her to feel the softness of his full lips. That's original Debby thought.

They sat for a while getting acquainted while sipping a bottle of Cristal that the owner sent over to Ty-Ran. Ty-Ran had invited Debby to join him at a private booth in the VIP section.

"I came here with a friend. I can't bounce on her," Debby said looking around for her girlfriend.

"She can come too," Ty-Ran said.

Debby found her and they followed Ty-Ran to the booth. Ty-Ran sat next to Debby and spoke in her ear over the sound of the Notorious B.I.G's voice booming in the club. Debby's friend flirted with guys as she sat alone at the table hoping to get a prize catch like Debby got.

"Hey Ty-Ran I ain't know they let ugly bitches in VIP." Ty-Ran, Debby and her girlfriend heard come out the mouth of a short, thick light skinned girl who accompanied by two other very pretty, voluptuous model looking females that approached the booth. Debby's girlfriend Tasha looked at the light-skinned girl up and down with a menacing frown.

"Bitch I know you ain't talking bout nobody at the table," Tasha barked.

"Don't take it personal. You ain't the only ugly bitch at this table," The light skin girl said creating laughter from her two person confidants. Debby began to remove her earrings and stood up coming face to face with the antagonizers.

"Uh uh bitch you got me fucked up," Debby growled. Ty-Ran stood up in between the group of females in an attempt to diffuse the situation.

"Ty-Ran you betta tell these bitches something cuz it's about to get real ugly in here," Debby continued.

"Yo Tracy fuck is you doing? You don't disrespect nobody you see me sitting with you hear me? Now take humpty and dumpty and yo self and find some clown niggas to buy you drinks or something." Ty-Ran scolded holding Debby's hand as he stood in between Debby and the girl. With his other hand he held Tasha back who already had her shoes off and had placed her earrings in her purse.

"It's like that Ran? I thought we were better than that." The light skin girl said embarrassed and flustered at Ty-Ran attitude.

"Yeah it's like that. Show some class next time. Beat it!" Ty-Ran ordered. The trio walked away with long faces.

"Ya'll sit down. Don't sweat them dumb bitches," Ty-Ran said to Debby and Tasha who sat down but didn't put their earring back on and Tasha left her shoes off just in case.

Ty-Ran thought to himself if Debby was in a mood to continue their night at his crib or anywhere private, that confrontation just messed that up. Debby looked pissed. "Who was that one of your little girlfriends?" Debby asked. Ty-Ran could sense her attitude.

"Nah. Some chicks I know from Roosevelt projects. The light skin one's brother is my homey. I ain't gonna lie I dealt with her a while ago but that's old news."

Debby had a friend from Roosevelt projects that she boosted with. Sometimes Debby would stop at that friend's apartment returning from a day of boosting to get rid of some of the stolen merchandise in Roosevelt. Debby made a mental note to ask her friend about this Tracy bitch and if possible get a chance to get a one on one fight with the loud mouth little heifer.

Ty-Ran knowing that Debby and Tasha came to the club by cab, offered them a ride home. They agreed whole-heartedly. Who could refuse a free ride? Plus, Debby wanted to see what Ty-Ran was pushing.

Just as Debby nerves were calmed after the confrontation and her mind was no longer on the girl from Roosevelt projects with the big mouth, outside in front of the club was the girl Tracy and what looked like the entire Roosevelt projects with her. Debby looked at her friend Tasha who was once again taking her earrings and shoes off saying, "This bitch thinks its sweet, oh it's on."

"A yo chill shorty ain't gonna be nothing. Ya'll with me. A yo Tracy what I told yo stupid ass?" Ty-Ran yelled to Tracy who was now dressed in a gray sweat suit with a scarf on her head and Vaseline on her face as was some of the other girls with her. There were even girls there holding babies in their arms.

"Fuck that shit Ran these bitches ain't gonna act like they want it and don't get it!" Tracy snarled.

"You know what Ty-Ran let me beat this bitch ass..." Debby said. Then she heard a familiar voice come from within the Roosevelt crowd.

"Debby? That's my girl Debby?" Debby recognized her boosting friend from Roosevelt walking towards her.

"Oh hell nah Tracy this is my girl. Wassup

Deb what happened?" Debby's tall dark skinned friend asked. Debby could tell that her friend was coming to fight too, and Debby knowing this girl knew that she most likely had a razor with her and she would use it.

"Wassup Steph? Naw this chick came out of nowhere disrespecting me and my girl because we were chilling with Ran," Debby said. Her friend Stephanie looked at Tracy then gave a dirty look to Ty-Ran before saying to Debby in a low tone.

"The bitch on his dick. He don't even fuck with her she don't get it."

"Steph, I wanna fight her. Her mouth is crazy," Debby said.

Stephanie looked Debby in the eye and knew that Debby was serious. Stephanie knew what the results were gonna be. Stephanie saw both girls in action and she would bet the house on Debby whipping Tracy's ass.

Stephanie turned to the Roosevelt crowd and said. "Ain't gonna be no jumping in..."

Stephanie turned her intention of coming to back up Tracy, to a fight one on one.

Ty-Ran whispered in Debby's ear. "You got this gorgeous?" Right then and there Debby's feelings for him went up. He was ready to take up for her and it turned her on. She smiled confidently and whispered in his ear.

"I got this, and when I'm done I want you."

It took no more than two minutes for Debby to jump on Tracy's ass and beat her into submission. When Debby was done, Tracy's face looked like the crowd she bought with her jumped her. The only remnants of a fight that Debby had was a swollen knuckle from punching Tracy on her forehead and head too many times.

Ty-Ran watched as Debby's skirt that she lifted above her knees showing the thickness of her thighs. The flawless chocolate skin hugs her juicy, big round bottom and he felt a tingle between his legs. He couldn't wait to sample that. He was also turned on by her ferocity. He liked a girl with a heart and a girl that wasn't afraid to get her hands dirty once in a while. Debby found out that Ty-Ran was driving a 1997 black CL 600 Benz.

After dropping Tasha off in Brownsville, he and Debby got a room at a Hilton hotel by J.F.K airport. Seeing Debby naked and feeling her warm vaginal walls tighten itself around his brick hard member, Ty-Ran was in love. The next day Debby put a block on her phone and erased Web out of her life.

For the first two years Ty-Ran and Debby were pretty much a happy couple. Ty-Ran spoiled her with everything a girl wanted. Jewelry, fur and he spent a lot of time wining and dining her. In return, Ty-Ran never had to buy clothes. She boosted clothes for him every time she went out to do her thang, which was almost every day.

Three years into the relationship problems started occurring. First Debby got locked up in Ohio for which Ty-Ran bailed her out. She got caught boosting at an outlet. Ty-Ran didn't pick her up in Ohio he sent her money for a plane ticket. Debby accused him of being with another chick as the reason for not coming to pick her up.

Secondly, when Debby went to Ty-Ran's Red Hook apartment that he shared with his mother and two youngest sisters and brother she would find ripped condom packets in his room.

They didn't use condoms when they had sex. Ty-Ran would lie and say his cousin be using his room when he out of town and him being out of town was a major issue with Debby. She knew he was down south messing with those country girls who loved them some New York niggas.

Then five years into their off and on relationship a son was born. The birth of little Ty-Ran eased the tension between the couple and it even made their bond tighter. Ty-Ran couldn't be happier than to have the splitting image of himself. Seeing Ty-Ran doing the father thing turned Debby on and she catered to Ty-Ran's every need.

A year after Ty-Ran's birth, the problems started again and this time big Ty-Ran was the one in the wrong for a fact. Debby wouldn't see him for months at a time. He wouldn't even call to see how his son was doing. When he came and got his son, he would drop him off at his mother's house and never spend time with him. The only time he came to see Debby was to have sex and he'd be gone in the morning back out of town. After that, their relationship had been off and on until he was murdered.

***

"Is that too tight?" Liz asked Debby as she continued braiding Debby's hair.

"Nah it's cool. Did I tell you the cops said that Cornbread was a part of a burglary ring and that's why he got killed because he owed some guys he was dealing with money?" Debby asked.

Liz paused for a second thinking about why Jabbar was locked up.

"What happened?" Debby asked curious as to why Liz stopped.

"Nothing. It's just wild how Jabbar is locked up for the same thing. They said he was part of a burglary ring," Liz said.

"Yeah but Cornbread was part of a ring out of the Bronx," Debby said causing Liz to drop the comb she had in her hand.

"Now what? Don't tell me Jabbar was part of a ring in the Bronx too?" Debby said as if Liz was skeptical for no reason.

Liz stared at her wall in a daze replying, "Yeah he was.

Chapter 10

Diondre

Upon his release from the hospital, Diondre spent a month at home on bed rest. Deidre stayed home and nursed him back to his old self. Liz was left in charge of running the salon in Deidre and Diondre's absence. The whole time Diondre was on bed rest, he never once discussed the robbery. In fact, the day he came home he asked Deidre to hang his picture of Elijah Muhammad back on the wall to cover his safe. Deidre didn't place the picture there when Diondre was in the hospital instead she placed a large plant on the mantle beneath the safe.

"Liz has been a blessing Dre. She has opened the salon every day and ran things efficiently. I don't know what I would do without her," Deidre said to Diondre as she drove her Altima from their Fort-Greene brownstone on the way to the salon.

Diondre nodded his head as he stared out at the Brooklyn streets alive with people on their way to their destination. There were guys hanging in front of bodegas doing whatever young guys do on those corners, kids getting on school buses while back packing teenagers headed to their high schools. Police sirens blaring in the background while the sound of buses moving up and down the busy avenues became the sound track of the action on the street.

As much as Diondre loved the heartbeat of Brooklyn and the physical attraction to living there, he was no longer emotionally attached to his place of birth. That morning he woke out of a coma and the story of the robbery was relayed to him, he decided that Brooklyn was no longer the place for him or his unborn child and fiancé. Since he woke up his mood has been a solemn one.

"Welcome back, welcome back, welcome back, welcome back!" Liz and the people in the shop sang the tune of *Welcome Back Carter* as Diondre and Deidre entered the salon.

A glittered sign hung on the ceiling saying welcome home Diondre along with a table situated in the middle of the salon that held a large assortment of Soul food and desserts. For the first time in a month, Deidre saw a smile on Diondre's face.

While Diondre received hugs and welcome back greetings from everyone in the shop, Deidre felt a sharp pain coming from her stomach. Her first thought was the baby kicking. But the pain became more intense so she took a seat in one of the chairs. Deidre's movement didn't go unnoticed by Liz.

"Dee you okay?" Liz asked concerned.

"Yeah I'm okay. I think this baby just kicked the shit out of me maybe from the noise here. He's telling them to keep it down," Deidre said trying to catch her breath while joking.

"Take it easy girl cause ain't nobody here ready to deliver no baby," Liz returned a humorous comment.

Just then detective Gardener and Chamberlain the same detectives who questioned Deidre at the hospital and arrested Jabbar came waltzing in the salon. The place became eerily quiet as everyone noticed the detectives. Deidre's heart skipped a beat as she recognized the cops. Liz face became hot red as she recognized the cops who took Jabbar away from her.

"May we help you?" Diondre asked.

The detectives flashed their badges before saying, "Good morning Mister Taylor it's good to see you up and well," detective Gardener said cordially. After Diondre thanked him for the well wishes he asked "What can I do for you officers?"

"We're here to place your wife under arrest for..." Everyone in the shop quickly turned to Deidre after hearing her collapse on the floor.

"What! Wait Dee baby what's wrong? Someone call an ambulance!" Diondre yelled. The detectives called for an ambulance on their walkie-talkie while trying to help with Deidre's situation. Deidre condition made everyone forget what the detectives said about arresting her. Within minutes, Deidre still unconscious, was loaded into an ambulance and rushed to Brookdale hospital.

Hours later when Deidre finally came to, she felt soreness in her abdomen and a cold feeling surround her wrist. When she tried to move her hand to wipe her eyes she realized her hand was handcuffed to the bed. The clinking sound of the handcuffs banging against the bed-rail alerted detective Gardener who was seated outside the room.

"Mrs. Taylor how are you feeling?" Gardener asked standing next to the bed smiling at Deidre. Besides the drowsiness, Deidre was feeling, furious about being handcuffed.

"Why am I handcuffed is what I wanna know?" Deidre asked with anger in her tone.

"Oh yeah. Your under arrest for conspiring to commit the house invasion and robbery and assault on your BOYFRIEND," the detective put emphasis on boyfriend letting Deidre know his knowledge of her not being Diondre's wife.

Deidre sucked her teeth and rolled her eyes. "Please, now tell me what's this really about I ain't got time for games."

"This isn't a game Miss Knots. The guy you know as Jabbar told us everything. As we speak Mister Bennet is in Federal Custody giving up the beans on a lot of things and the robbery was one of them. We know everything. We know about you letting Mister Bennet and his accomplice in the house by turning the alarm off. We know you left the door open so they could enter and we know about yours and mister Bennet's sexual relationship. It's up to you Miss Knots to save yourself now."

Deidre's jaw almost hit the bed at hearing what Jabbar told the cops. *How could he? That bastard. This was all his fault. This was his plan and he black mailed me to do it. I should have never did it. I should have just came clean to Diondre and Liz.* Those consequences are better to deal with than a prison.

"He blackmailed me!" Deidre cried. "Where's

Diondre?"

"Miss Knott, Mister Taylor left after your operation," the detective said.

"What operation?" Deidre asked confused.

"You had a C-section. You gave birth to a premature baby boy." The detective informed her. Deidre was told that Diondre and Liz were made aware of the charges being brought against her. When they found out the whole story, Diondre stayed with the baby while Liz ran out of the hospital crying.

Deidre cried herself to sleep that night. The next morning via telephone-conference, she was arraigned and appointed a public defender. Her bail was set at fifteen thousand dollars.

***

Eighty year old Miss Daniel laid dead due to a severe heart attack after being frighten by the sound of a battering ram being used to crash through her door as police from the N.Y.P.D, ATF, U.S. Marshalls fugitive task force, and F.B.I agents entered her project apartment looking for Web.

Paramedics were called in to try to revive Miss Daniels but she gave up the ghost, as she would say, went home to her lord. Meanwhile Web got a call on his cell phone from a girl that lived in Miss Daniel's building while he drove his Yukon through the Bronx streets once again visiting Gaston home in Kingsbridge.

"They all over the place. Web I'm so sorry but Miss Dee had a heart attack when they ran up in there.

She's gone Web."

Web clicked off his cell phone and his hand gripped the steering wheel tightly as a tear flowed down his dark skin. He couldn't believe she was gone and it was his fault he told himself. I *brought this trouble to her door. Damn!* Web became angrier as he pictured her lying dead while a bunch of cops rummaged through the apartment. Then he pictured her always-smiling face. She was kind to everyone that came in contact with her. She fed the homeless people and even the prostitutes that hung around the projects.

Web remembered as a child when his mother, a heroine addicted prostitute, dropped him off at his grandmother's door and he never saw his mother again. His grandmother raised him like she gave birth to him herself. She was the only person alive that Web trusted and truly loved.

As he pulled up in front of the Kingsbridge home, Web pulled out his black colt 45 and screwed a silencer on it. He put the gun in the front pocket of his black hooded sweatshirt and stepped out into the rainy night quickly walking to the house. The living room window had a blinking glow from the T.V. being on. Web looked in the window and could see silhouettes through the white curtains. Miss Gaston sat on a love seat watching TV. Web knocked.

Miss Gaston looked out the window and Web smiled removing his hood from his head. Miss Gaston opened the door.

"Webster what's wrong baby you okay?" Miss Gaston said walking back to the living room.

"I was in the ...." Web finished his sentence after raising the gun to the back of Miss Gaston head and pulled the trigger. "Neighborhood and decided to pay you and the kid a visit." Web walked in Gaston's little brother's room and saw that he was sleep under a Pokeman blanket. Web walked over to the bed and pumped seven shots in the boy's body. The kid never felt a thing. Web did the deed as a payback to Lamar Gaston snitching on him. So he thought.

The morning after Deidre gave birth to her baby, Diondre and his family visited the hospital to see the baby. The baby was hooked up to tubes and machines in an incubator in the I.C.U. Diondre and his family stared behind a glass partition at the pale body that weighed 1 pound. Diondre's father hugged Diondre as he cried.

He couldn't understand why this was happening to him. What did he do to deserve this? He asked. And now his baby had to suffer. Diondre's anger resurfaced when he thought about Deidre's betrayal. Out of all people to betray him why did it have to be Deidre? Deidre wasn't supposed to turn out to be a scandal. She was his Candle, his everything, his Brooklyn woman. How could she, and for what a night of sex from a man who's dating her best friend. A man who lied about who he was and what he does? A man who could care less about her?

Now look, he's cooperating with the cops bringing her down to save himself.

"I'm gonna take a blood test," Diondre said to

his father.

"Whatever choice you make we are here for you," Mister Taylor said as the family joined in a group hug.

Chapter 11

Liz

"Today this community mourns the loss of one of its long time residents, friend, mother. A god fearing kind woman who suffered a massive heart attack after police stormed her apartment looking for a criminal who doesn't live there. Eighty year old Etta Mae Daniel's body will make its way through her Canarsie neighborhood and will be laid to rest at the Evergreen Cemetery." A reporter said as crowds of residents of Bruekelen projects lined the streets yelling 'No Justice No Peace' while a funeral procession consisting of two limousines carrying family members of Miss Daniels, family and friends in their own vehicles all lead by the black hearse carrying the body of the kind loving woman.

There were tears in many people's eyes as swarms of media and police on foot and in vehicles joined in the procession. The police were there to keep the crowd under control just in case an uprising occurred. There were a lot of expressions of rage and anger yelled from the crowd aimed at the police.

"The police say they were serving a fugitive warrant on Miss Daniels grandson, a Webster Daniels wanted by state and Federal authorities on various charges including robbery and murder.

Daniels is an ex-con currently on parole after serving ten years for a murder committed in this very neighborhood. Police say they got a tip that Daniels was hiding out at his grandmother's apartment but according to officials at the New York state Department of parole, Daniels was not paroled to this address nor was his name on the lease. Community activists are saying that the police should have knocked before busting in on that woman. An investigation is pending." The reporter commented as the procession passed.

Web drove in a small brown Dotsun with tinted windows behind the funeral procession. It didn't matter to him that the cops were on his trail. Nothing would stop him from seeing his grandmother buried. He had to say his last words to her. When the crowd of mourners began to make their way to the burial site, Web wearing a black suit, with a black shirt and tie, blended in the crowd. He wore a five o-clock shadow and covered his head with a black Fedora hat and wore a pair of shades to disguise himself. He patted the two 45's he had in holsters on both sides of the arms as an assurance to himself that if the cops tried to get him he would give them a hell of a hard time catching him.

There was so much media and people that nobody noticed Web. The only person that noticed him was Debby. As Debby stood by a tree waiting for the pastor to give the eulogy Web noticed her. They locked eyes for a few seconds, Web smiled at her and Debby looked away. *This nigga got a lot of nerve being here when he got the whole goddamn army looking for him. His crazy gay ass probably up to something anyway. They're going to kill Web and it would do a lot of us a favor. Poor Miss Daniels died cause this nigga selfish bullshit. Then he gonna smile at me. Nigga please!* Debby thought to herself.

"The lord giveth and the lord taketh...!" A pastor spoke standing behind a podium on front of the black casket. Web looked around nervously listening to the pastor. Once in a while he would sneak a glance at Debby who would roll her eyes every time she caught him looking.

"A few days ago he took back one of his most loyal servants. He told us ya'll can't have her no more!" the pastor's words became animated. "She is mines to have. Ya'll had her eighty years now. Her time to be with God eternally has come!"

Debby saw Web's head jerk in the direction of a few trees away from the mourners. Debby looked in the same direction and she saw what made Web look. A white man dressed in Jeans and a black turtleneck covered by a black vest stood behind a tree. Web looked all around and saw more cops taking up positions behind trees, mausoleums and grave stones. Debby didn't understand why Web had a grin on his face knowing they were there for him. Then she saw him reach in his jacket and removed the two guns. "Ah shit this nigga gonna act a fool up in here," Debby said to herself. Debby started to walk away in the opposite direction on her way to the exit the cemetery.

"Etta, May god..." the pastor's words were cut off by the sound of gun fire. Boc! Boc! Boc! Boc!

Web ran backwards while aiming at the cops behind gravestones and trees. He was headed towards his car. People in the crowd screamed and ducked as the cops return fire.

Rat! Tat! Tat! Rat! Tat! Tat! Boom! Boom! Boc! Boc!

Web ducked behind a Mausoleum getting out of the way of the rapid fire coming from the cops assault rifles and handguns. He knew he had to run as fast as he could to get to his car because he only had two clips and they were almost empty.

Waiting to catch his breath, Web looked from behind the Mausoleum to see if the cops were moving forward. When he saw they stayed in their initial positions he made a quick dash towards his car shooting the guns behind him as he ran. When his guns emptied he tossed them and stayed low as the cops fired.

Web's legs gave out and he collapsed before he got to the car. He didn't feel the bullets from an AR-15 hit him in the legs. He realized he was hit once he tried to get up. "Don't fucking move Daniels or I'll finish you right here!" Web laid down and didn't move. Debby watched from her rented Cherokee as the cops cuffed a wounded Web. She shook her head and giggled.

"Got his sorry ass. That nigga ain't ever coming home again," Debby turned on her stereo and let Beyonce voice fill the car. "Let me upgrade you."

***

"Fuck you mean six hundred dollars. This is a D-class V.V.S diamond with a platinum setting. The ring alone is more than a thousand dollars!" Liz yelled to a fat pale white man behind the glass partition of a pawnshop.

"I looked at the diamond it has a lot of flaws, it's not V.V.S. someone lied to you doll," the man said wiping his sweaty forehead with a dirty handkerchief. "I'll give you nine hundred, final offer."

Liz was furious. People always tryna get over on people from the hood. They think all ghetto people are stupid. Like we wouldn't know something authentic from the fake. They think everything we buy is a knock-off. Sorry honey but a lot of us know our shit. *This white bastard is lucky I could care less about the ring Jabbar's no good trifling ass brought and Deidre oh my god. If I could get my hands on that back stabbing bitch right now. Oh man she just don't know. Damn she is foul. She's going to set Diondre up for some dick. What type of shit she on? Liz* thought to herself.

"You know what you con artist bastard. I'll take the nine but don't think I don't know about this shit. I know V.V.S when I see it." Liz handed him the ring through a small open space, in the fiber glass partition.

Liz also needed the money to pay bills. Since the whole ordeal with Deidre's arrest, Diondre hasn't opened the salon and things were tight. Liz even resorted back to boosting.

Something surprisingly Debby tried to talk her

out of.

"Just look for a job. I got some applications for you," Debby said one day as they sat in Liz kitchen drinking E and J.

"Debby please, with that theft charge on my record ain't nobody hiring my thieving ass," Liz said with Debby nodding in agreement.

"I know exactly what you mean," Debby replied.

The last time Liz spoke to Diondre he told her he didn't know what he was going to do about the shop. Liz wanted to say don't close it. There was a lot of money being made there and if he let her she would make sure it opened everyday and ran it thoroughly. Instead, she said nothing. She knew Diondre was going through a lot. To make matters worse he found out that the baby that Deidre had wasn't his and that the baby was HIV positive. Meaning Deidre was infected possibly by Jabbar. Liz immediately took the test and was waiting for the results. Diondre got his results back and he was negative. Lucky him.

Still in all with the good heart Diondre has he felt there was no need for the child to suffer because of some irresponsible parent. Diondre decided he would adopt the child who he named Shamar Cornelius Taylor after his two childhood friends.

Diondre thought about what Shamar would say in all this mess. He even heard Shamar's voice in his head. "I told you Brooklyn broads are mainly scandals. Even the ones that front like they are goody, goody." And Diondre knew Cornbread would agree with Shamar.

Epilogue

When Liz received the result of her AID's test the news was devastating. She was HIV positive. Liz fell into a deep depression for months. It wasn't until Diondre, Debby, and friends from the salon went to her apartment and showed their support by promising to be there for her through her dilemma that she started to come out of her funk. Diondre surprised her by handing her keys and a stack of papers. "Welcome aboard partner." He made Liz co-owner of the salon which he changed its name to L & D's. Liz couldn't be happier.

Even more surprising to Liz is when one day Debby revealed to her. "I fucked Diondre."

"What!" Liz said astonished.

Debby had a mischievous grin on her face. "He couldn't refuse this big ass I threw at him."

"Girl you ain't shit." Liz retorted. "How was it?" Liz asked causing her and Debby to burst out laughing. "Deidre fucked up big time!"

For her testimony, Deidre was sentenced to five years probation. She moved into a shelter in Brooklyn after applying for welfare, being that she spent the majority of her savings paying court fines and restitution for the money Diondre lost.

In exchange for his testimony, Jabbar was sentenced to ten years concurrent with his ten year sentence he received in the Federal Courts. He is currently serving that sentence at The Clinton Correction facility in Danemora New York under protective custody. Strangely even in protective custody he was somehow cornered in the showers and raped repeatedly. He is now the bitch of an inmate from the Canarsie section of Brooklyn.

Gaston testified at Jabbar's federal trial. Before Jabbar's trial Gaston was informed about the brutal murders of his mother and brother. He broke down crying telling the Marshalls; "It was Webster who did it. He threatened me in a letter. He said if I snitched that would happen. I didn't snitch on him. He lied to me!"

Web was sentenced in state court to life in prison without parole. Web growled at the judge who sentenced him. "Take your life sentence and stick it in your kids' asses like I'm going to do if I see them."

Web was led out the courtroom by court officer to an awaiting couple of detectives.

"Webster Daniels, the detectives announced.

"Yo get the fuck outta my face pigs!" Web snarled.

"You are being placed under arrest for the double murder of Lora Gaston and Jeffrey Gaston."

Web was sent upstate to Attica after being arraigned on the new murder charges. In Attica Web got back to his old routine of prison life.

He extorted, raped and intimidated the weak until one day karma showed up at his cell in the form of a group of Puerto Rican inmates led by a skinny guy who looked familiar to Web.

"Yo remember me duke?" The skinny guy asked.

Web stood up and walked towards the entrance of his cell. "Am I supposed to remember you?" Web's posture was one that didn't say he was nervous though he was. He could tell by the group's demeanor that this meeting wasn't going to be cordial. He knew the guys were Latin Kings and particularly the ones at his cell door were known leaders of the gang and vicious cats.

"Greenhaven the year 2000," the skinny guy retorted.

The group didn't give Web a chance to go for his weapon he had connected to a thin string that hung out of his toilet. They were on him with their shanks stabbing him until he stopped moving. Web laid there with a six inch fiber glass shank sticking out of his forehead. To totally disrespect Web, the skinny guy stood over him and urinated on Web's face.

After putting the Fort Greene Brownstone on the market, Diondre sold within a year's time. He quickly moved into a modest one-story home in Valley Stream Long Island where he and his adopted son Shamar spent creating a bond that Diondre knew wouldn't be broken by lies, deceit and betrayal. Diondre's family began to visit the city often spending time with him and Shamar. The family adored Shamar and filled his fragile life with love and care. His HIV status was kept in check by the continuing plan of eating right and his medication. Diondre made sure of that. When Shamar got old enough to understand things more clearly, he would explain the situation about Deidre, Diondre decided. Until then the women in his life were his sisters, Liz and...

Diondre dialed a number on his cell phone as he sat on his king-size bed covered in silk Versace sheets. When the person answered, Diondre smiled hearing the sexy voice. "Hey baby what you wearing right now?" Diondre asked in a seductive voice.

"Nothing." Debby answered. Debby moved into her own apartment in a nice section of far Rockaway Queens after Diondre helped her to get a job at a restaurant called Amy Ruth's in Harlem. Diondre knew the owners for a while.

After the trial Diondre pulled Debby to the side and expressed his regret of his past treatment towards her. "Listen Debby, I've misjudged you in the past like I did Liz she could tell you. I want to apologize for being prejudge mental and if..."

Debby cut him off.

"Dre you don't owe me an apology. I would have prejudged me too. I mean I was living life like there was no tomorrow. You're a good man Dre and you deserve much better than what you've been going through," Debby said.

"Stop it Debby. No one's perfect. We could all use a makeover. Let me take you to dinner?" Diondre said surprising Debby, with that brief conversation, started a friendship that came with some benefits.

"You up for a night cap. I'll pay for the cab,"

Diondre said changing channels with his remote.

"You know I'm up for it," Debby replied. "I was just reading this book and it got me horny as hell. You should read it."

"Well bring it over here and I'll read it after I read you," Diondre said in a sexy voice.

"Okay baby. But serious this book is banging," Debby said.

"What's it called?" Diondre asked.

"It's called Brooklyn Sexy."

Peace

ABOUT THE AUTHOR

Myles Ramzee describes himself as, a "tale of two boroughs" born in Brooklyn, New York raised in the streets of Jamaica Queens and Brooklyn. Growing up in a Muslim household Myles parents in still in him manners, discipline and respect for himself and others. Life hasn't always been easy for him both parents were former drug addicts they separated when he was at the age of 6. As Myles reached his teenage years he searched for a father figure he turned to the streets to find one in hustlers and gangsters that ran his neighborhood. Myles constantly struggles within himself the battle of being a hoodlum and being a righteous Muslim.

Once his mother became a fully fledged lesbian she and her manipulative lover sold drugs. Myles mother constantly scolded him for staying in the streets. That's what pushed Myles further into the streets. Myles sold drugs on the streets of South Jamaica. He also robbed and sold drugs on the streets of Brooklyn that cause him to go in and out of jail.

At the age of 23 years old Myles life change forever when the U. S. Marshalls came and raided his Bruekelen apartment for a murder of a man who was associated with friend of his. Myles eventually was locked up in Pennsylvania for a murder he didn't commit and was falsely accused. He was framed and evidences were manufactured along with deceit and lies of a female Caucasian drug addict who implicated him and three of Myles friends in the crime. An all white jury in Carbon Country, Pennsylvania found him and his friends guilty and sentence them all to life without parole. Presently Myles continue to fight for his innocence and his freedom.

Myles has completely changed his life for the better good. He is actively involved in a mentor program where he and several other men incarcerated lecture teens to keep them on the right track.

Enjoy these other books. Urban Fiction at its best.

BROOKLYN SEXY PART 1   **$10.99**

In almost every city in America, women are stereo typed based on the sections or neighborhood they came from. The five boroughs of New York City are like five different cities in one. They are close in proximity and in a lot of ways they are worlds apart.

Brooklyn, the most populated borough, probably has the city's worst reputation when it comes to people, in particular to men of the boroughs. Brooklyn women have the reputation of being seen tough, mean spirited and conniving money hungry thieves who set up men to be robbed by Brooklyn stick up kids. Diondre, a Brooklyn born and raised entrepreneur has two best friends from Harlem who feel as if all Brooklyn women fit the stereotype. Diondre sets out to prove them wrong.

When Diondre meets Deidre, a girl he met in high school. Deidre knocks the stereotype out of Prospect Park. Sadly one of Diondre's best friends doesn't live to see it. The mean streets of Brooklyn claim his life to which the other friend develops a disdain for the borough known as, "Buck Town."

As Diondre defends Brooklyn women he is shocked to find out that his woman is exactly what his friends claim Brooklyn women are like. Deidre's deep dark secret comes to light. He learns this heart breaking news at the cost of a close friend life. Brooklyn Sexy Part 1 and 2 is a tale of betrayal, infidelity, sex, robbery, karma, murder and love. It's truly a Brooklyn Story.

FLIPPIN' THE GAME 3 $15.99

After the convictions and deaths of the Black Top Crew hierarchy, Keenan Giles Junior sets out to clear his family name and build a relationship with the last of the Classon clan, Malik. Malik, now more mature and meeting the love of his life wants out of the game. Keenan Junior thinks Malik is getting weak and seeks to get rid of all the Classons will not let another family member tarnish the bloodline.

SOUTH PHILLY CHICK 1 (The Epitome of Loyalty) $15.99

Tina Tee White take you through the journey of her life as a young black girl, into her adult years as a South Philly chick, going through stages of three lovers tied to a life of crime. From burglary, to shop lifting, credit card scams, drug abuse, robberies, set ups, and murders, she lives it all.

She meet the love her life, Mar. Their love affair can be viewed in the pages of a fairy tale (with murders and kidnapping). Tee brings to life the myth of the South Philly Chick. Through her loyalty, trust, and unconditional love for her man; a ruthless and psychopathic murderer;

they exemplify the Hood's new Bonnie and Clyde. But will they live happily ever after? You'll find out, but not in the first of this trilogy.

SOUTH PHILLY CHICK 2: (The Keys to the City)   **$15.99**

Once again, Mar and Tee, South Philly's King and Queen return. After being saved by Mar, life goes on. The city of Philadelphia's underworld is given to Mar on a silver platter, but with that platter comes betrayal, death and deceit.

Mar tries his hand at something new. La Cosa Nostra boss Don Salvatore Bellini will give Mar the keys to the city. Will this historical event be a successful one?

When the riches are presented, hatred, jealousy, envy and betrayal are sure to follow it.

Once again, Tee proves to be the epitome of loyalty like the ride or die chick she is. If you enjoyed Volume I, you will love Vol. II. Now sit back and enjoy the ride of one of the hardest street savvy visionaries. Big Snoop doesn't just write, he recollects!

Millennium Black Millionaires   **$15.99**

The city of Philadelphia is flood with ruthless gangsters and killers. The infamous M.B.M. family goes from being dead broke hustling in the streets to living a lavish life style that is only seen in the movies.

Everything changes for them when Sasaladine meets Alicia and she introduces him to corporate hustling. Just as they start making the transition from the streets to go corporate, their past come back to haunt them and Sasaladine is arrested for a homicide.

Franchise is the loose cannon of the crew and will kill at the drop of a dime. He has his own plans on taking over the streets of Philly by force but he runs into a problem with Tameka and Mario, two females that are just as trigger happy as him and are ready for war.

Rasul and Naim work hard at trying to leave the street life alone but can't resist splurging on nice things now that they have money.

They are all taken by surprise when the F.B.I. moves in and arrest a key member of the M.B.M. and puts everything that they worked hard for at risk.

Will they be able to live out their dreams or will they spend the rest of their days in Federal lock up? You will find out but not in the first of a trilogy.

Millennium Black Millionaires 2: The City of Brotherly Love $15.99

The Millennium Black Millionaires are back by popular demand. Marlo and Tameka are up to their old tricks again when they head to the Bad Landz looking for a new place to distribute their cocaine. An all about war occurs when they bump into Belinda and Maidi two Spanish females with just as much money and heart as them.
Alicia and Babia start to learn their way around Philly and fall in love

with the upbeat pace of the city while Kasha and Patrice work hard at trying to be successful but loses focus once Rasheeda introduces them to credit card scams.

Just when they start to see life changing results. Everything comes to a halt and one of the girls is killed during a botched robbery. Will the girls be successful at finding the right loop holes in the streets?

You will find out but not in the second book of the trilogy.

BLACK OPT'S DIVISION (BETRAYAL) DECEIT OF THE HIP-HOP WORLD $15.00

Black Opt's Division takes you deep inside Philadelphia's underworld of drugs, dope-money and murder. It exposes the hidden agenda of certain government branches and their insincerity of intentions towards the African American race. Yet it's filled with enough swagger for "Hollywood." This book will captivate the mind with its intense violent scenes and exquisite sex scenes.

While exposing the F.B.I. conspiracy with drugs in Philadelphia, it explains how Feds manipulate the streets with informers. Last but not least, the romance love scene between J-Sizzle and Kema will leave you in tears. A tale of sex, murder, Hip-Hop, bad bitches and coke.......

More Great Reads Coming Soon

Millennium Black Millionaires 3
South Philly Chick III
Heir To The Throne Trilogy
DA-M (Born to Win) The Realest Hood Tale Neva Told

Mail This Order Form to:

Angel Eyes Publications
P. O. Box 22031
Beachwood, Ohio 44122

	QTY	PRICE
Brooklyn Sexy Part 1	_____	$10.99
Brooklyn Sexy Part 2	_____	$10.99
Flippin' The Game 3	_____	$15.99
Millennium Black Millionaires 1	_____	$15.99
Millennium Black Millionaires 2	_____	$15.99
Black Opt's Division Betrayal	_____	$15.99
South Philly Chick I	_____	$15.99
South Philly Chick II	_____	$15.99

Add 3.95 for each book for Shipping and Handling
We ship to prisons... State, County and Federal

Name_____

Address _____

State_____ City_____ Zip _____

Angel Eyes Publications and H. S. P. Publications
Thank You For Your Business

BROOKLYN SEXY PART 2

MYLES RAMZEE

CPSIA information can be obtained at www.ICGtesting.com
Printed in the USA
LVOW04s2240290715

448121LV00010B/178/P

9 780692 314739